# Jake's
# REDEMPTION

## A MEMORIES NOVEL
# JEAN KELSO

JEAN KELSO
*Jake's Redemption*
© 2016 Jean Kelso
All Rights Reserved

Cover by CJPB Designs
Editing & Interior Design: Fancy Pants Book Formatting
Paperback ISBN: 978-0-9951929-5-9
eBook ISBN: 978-0-9951929-4-2

# DEDICATION

To Doreen, and Shannon. You are my rocks ladies. Always there when I need you. Thank you. This is for you!

JEAN KELSO

# ACKNOWLEDGMENTS

For starters I want to say thank you to everyone who requested more from these characters. I enjoyed writing more of this story. Jake may have been bad to the bone at one point, but there tends to be a good side in all of us.

I want to start by thanking you, my readers for taking the time out of your day to read this book. Without you, there would be no one out there to enjoy my story.

Thank you to my family and friends for always being by my side. I love you.

To my beta team, you are amazing. Shannon, Amy, and Leddy. Your input towards the story helped me pull everything together, so thank you.

To Casey Harvell. You are da bomb girl. Last minute, short notice, you are always there. THANK YOU! Your business Fancy Pants Formatting is amazing! This girl rocked my edits and my formatting. She helped me with so much, love you, girl!

To Chelsea Barnes at CJPB Designs. You rock my friend. Thank you so much for my amazing cover.

Thank you, thank you, thank you to everyone and anyone out there who supports my writing and stories. Your love and support means so much to me!

JEAN KELSO

# CONTENTS

# PROLOGUE

*Jake*

Being behind bars alone and having to fight for yourself days on end gets tiresome. The nights are the hardest to deal with, leaving me with too much time to just sit and think of all the shit I've done in my life. The people I've hurt, and those I've killed. The many lives I have ruined.

How cruel of a man I became under my father's thumb. It was all I knew. Even being in here—this big-ass prison—Connor Green's thugs think they can run my life, threatening me, pushing me into fights…even going as far as intimidating me for when (or if) I ever get parole. But it's all words. Endless, useless words that mean nothing since they can't do anything without their boss's say. And their boss hasn't said boo to me since we got sentenced.

With the shakedown between Simon (my father's right-hand man) and my brother, Sean, all the lies were revealed about my family and the so called business. The drugs, guns, and murders. They have seriously affected me and I don't know if I want to be that misguided man anymore.

I have no idea how to change—how to go from a drug-running, gun-slinging, bad-ass enforcer, to a good, honest man.

I guess I'll just have to serve my time, and figure that shit out later.

JEAN KELSO

# CHAPTER ONE

*Jake*

I can't believe I survived seven long-ass years in hell. I was sentenced for ten. Getting early parole was pure luck. After I was able to get a few things straightened out—like the constant fighting with other inmates who came at me—all I did was keep to myself and tried to do all that I was told by my superiors.

Inside those cold, concrete walls, time was never-ending. All I could do was think. Think about all the crap I'd done and what a horrible person I was. It didn't take me long, but when I realized I didn't want to be that man anymore—the man my father made me into—I did what I had to do. I smartened up and behaved to the best of my ability. I survived. It was my best option if I wanted to get out alive.

Dad and Simon are still in custody, for which I'm thankful for. You see, those men ruled the roost. I'd watched them beat men into submission—better men than me—more times than I could count. Like I said, I hate the man I became.

My brother Dominic (who used to be thick as thieves with me when we were kids) is nowhere to be found. At least, that's what we were told when we went to trial. I'm sure the police aren't looking very hard for him anymore, anyways. He was always a sneaky bastard. He's probably in a whole other country living it up, not giving two shits about the rest of us. No, but really—he's probably worrying about us, but worrying more about not getting caught. You see, Dom is a good five years older than me. The great Connor Green was able to get his claws into him sooner, so Dom has a few rougher edges than the rest of us. But, hey—he's my brother and I love him. And miss him, too.

11

## JEAN KELSO

So here I stand in the middle of this beat down, rat's ass, cheap motel room. The first thing I need to do is shower and sleep. I haven't had a good night's sleep in years. Showering with guards around and sleeping with one eye open does nothing for a person trying to survive. It takes so much out of you.

The prison gave me the clothing I was sentenced in, freshly laundered. It's a good thing my weight didn't really change while inside or I would've had a problem. My old Doc Martens looked almost brand new. I place them on the counter in the tiny bathroom and begin to strip out of the filthy prison rags, the gray joggers and plain white tee shirt I have on. I'm glad they let me leave wearing the ugly things. I didn't want to put my clean clothes on feeling like the trash I am.

Standing stark naked, I look in the dirty mirror and gaze over my ragged body. Tattoos cover a portion of my upper body, along with some old hardly noticeable scars. I tried to not let myself go while in the slammer, but I'm ashamed of the new scars that mark my body. In the beginning of my sentence, I had to fight. Everyone was always in my face—inmates, my superiors, enemies. But like I mentioned, when I realized what I wanted I moved forward. Shaking my weary head, I turn toward the tiny shower. I turn the water on hot and step under, leaning my arms on the cold tiles in front of me to rest my head on them and let the water fall over my tired body.

Damn, does it ever feel good for my body to relax under the cascading warm waterfall all alone for the first time in seven years where there isn't anyone watching me. My muscles begin to loosen up area by area—neck, shoulders, back. My cloudy mind eases and I feel like I can finally breathe for the first time in my life.

After I soak in as much heat as possible, my muscles feel like goo. I suppose it's time to soap up and get out. After a quick rub down, I rinse off, grab a towel and step out into the steam-filled room. I wipe the dirty mirror with my hand and stare myself down. Disgust. Regrets. That's what I see staring back. I blow a breath out and begin to dry off. I'm so disappointed with myself for how my life turned out. I'm thirty-five years old and have nothing to show for the life I have lived except a rap sheet and a prison term. My regrets are a list a mile long, and on the top of it's my brother Sean. But first, I need to deal with me before I can deal with anything else. I need to get my head above water, tread lightly and stay afloat before I can start making amends for the shit I've done.

I'm exhausted. Slipping on my briefs, I leave the rest of my clothing on the counter and head toward the bed. I don't even bother pulling the blankets back—I just flop on top, pull the pillow under my head, and close my eyes. I know sleep will take me fast. After a good night's rest, I'll start figuring shit out.

I wake up surrounded by darkness. I guess my little nap turned into a full-blown sleep. I turn my head to look at the clock on the nightstand and it is eight o'clock in the evening. Damn. I roll over and sit on the side of the bed. Rubbing the sleep out of my eyes, it dawns on me. I've been out of jail for a whole twelve hours and haven't had a damn thing to eat yet. As if it heard me thinking, my stomach growls.

Standing from the bed I stretch, working every kink possible out of my tired muscles and head toward the bathroom. I wash my face and brush my teeth with the cheap tooth brush and paste I picked up on the way here and get dressed. I run my hands through my short brown hair and know I'm set. I need to get some food. Real food. After consuming seven years of prison food, I'm surprised I survived.

I remember passing a little diner a few doors down from the motel. Things sure have changed around here over the years. I'm not ready for a night out in the city, so a little place is just perfect. I grab my wallet, put my shoes on, lock up with the key they gave me and head out to satisfy my hunger.

It's a calm, warm evening for May. The smell of rain is in the air. I walk the short distance to the place I remember seeing. I stop in front and look up at the sign. Granny's Diner. Hmph. Typical name for a little Podunk place. I laugh to myself and open the door. The intoxicating smell is the first to hit. Fresh home-cooked food. Damn, my mouth is watering. I look around, the place is pretty busy. There's a wooden bar, full of patron's drinking, and booths surrounding three walls. A few modest tables sit in the middle, and music plays just loud enough to be heard. Not bad.

There's no one there to seat me, so I assume it's a seat-yourself establishment. Looking for a place to sit, I move farther into the diner. The smell of the food makes my stomach grumble loudly, and I can't wait to sink my teeth into something delicious.

Sitting in a corner booth, I flip open a menu. As I start reading the specials a small shadow appears over me.

"Did you want to start off with a drink?" The sweetest, softest voice in the room asks.

I look up to see the cutest little blonde my eyes have ever laid eyes on. Short hair, bright pale blue eyes and a smile so big, her teeth sparkled. I'm literally stunned. It's not because of the fact that I haven't seen a beautiful woman for seven years—it's that the woman looks like an angel looking down on me, offering me her salvation instead of food.

I clear my throat and shake my thoughts. "Yes, please." I smile. My rugged looks of short brown hair and gray eyes may not be overly pleasing to everyone's eyes, but I used to be a looker. At least the women used to tell me so.

My beautiful angel licks her lips and begins to tap her notepad. "Well, what will it be?" She smiles again.

Damn, I must look like a fool. Am I just staring at her? Fuck me, I'm an idiot. I swallow deeply. "Can I get a Coke, please?"

"You sure can, hot stuff." She quickly writes it down and walks away.

Holy fuck in heaven. Is this a sign or am I just wishing for way too much in this life? This can't be that easy can it? No, she is just a waitress in a diner and I'm a fucking fool that is horny as hell. Yep, that's it.

I pick up the menu again and continue looking over the options.

JEAN KELSO

# CHAPTER TWO

*Devon*

Oh, my God—that was Jake Green. I thought he was in jail. A tingle shivers up my spine. I haven't seen him since high school. Well, he wasn't exactly in school at the time. He's older than me by a few years—but he hung around outside with friends, and his brother was in class with me. I knew who he was because of Sean. Plus, I saw him around some of the girls from school. I always thought he was hot. Too good-looking for his own good. Cocky, you could say. I'll admit I sort of liked him.

He has no idea who I am. He never really did. Nobody really did back then, but that's beside the point. And now, here he is. I take a deep breath. Reaching into the cooler, I pull out the Coke he asked for and reach for a glass to pour it into. Fucking Jake Green. A murderer—according to the news—In my diner. Well, not my diner—but the diner I work in. I don't know how to feel about him being here.

I followed the news, the trial, everything that happened seven years ago. I knew that family was bad—not the whole family—but I never expected murder to be on that list. Even with the rumors I heard about his crazy-ass dad.

I should be scared. Yes, that's it. Terrified. I better stop flirting. Why the hell am I flirting? I can get into some serious trouble. I'm a good girl, I don't need trouble. I heard what he did to his own brother. Sean. Fuck. Ugh.

I put ice in the glass, and slowly pour the Coke on an angle to prevent too much foam to build up. Taking a deep breath to contain myself, I walk back over to him. I set the drink down and pull my notepad from my pocket.

17

"Have you decided?" I ask him. I hope he doesn't notice the inner turmoil I fight over being so close to him.

He closes the menu and looks up to me with a smile. Damn that smile. That's a dangerous smile. I bite my tongue. He's bad. I just keep breathing. This is bad.

"I'll have a burger with the works and a side of fries, please."

I nod at him with a small smile. "Coming right up." And I walk away. Fuck, that wasn't easy. We get a variety of people in here, but criminals from the news? Not often. But it's only Jake. Maybe that's why I haven't freaked the fuck out.

I head into the kitchen to place his order with the cook, Mark.

I don't know why this guy twists me up so bad. He's really no one to me. Maybe it's because he just got out of prison for a whole lot of bullshit that makes me just want to scream. He looks better than he did in school—and when I say better, I mean fucking hot. They say people can change. Fuck! Why the fuck was I so nice to him? I need to stop flirting. Ugh, I hate my fucking life. I can't be that hard up, can I?

I'm twenty-nine years old and still living in the same damn place I grew up in. I do have my own home (bonus for me!) I worked my ass off for it, but the city remains the same. I'm single and working in a silly diner that I've worked in since high school. I didn't go to college because I was an idiot and I just keep making mistakes in life. I don't know if I'll ever have my happily ever after.

"Yo, Dev! Order up!" Mark calls out.

Another order's ready for me to serve. I head over to the counter and pick it up. I check the tab to see which table and head over. Putting a smile on my face, I set the plate down. "Can I get you anything else?" I ask the old man sitting alone at the table.

"No, mam." He utters.

"Well, be sure to holler if you need something." I smile and walk away.

Back in the kitchen, I watch quietly, sort of in a daze while Mark flips burgers and does other food prep. My mind just isn't in it tonight. Well, it was until Jake walked in and turned it into a pile of confused crap.

"What's up, baby girl?" Mark asks.

I blow out a breath. "Can you believe I have worked here for twelve years Mark? Twelve fucking years." I slump back on the counter and sigh.

"Come on, baby girl. I thought you loved working here."

I look up to Mark, who has been a great friend for like ever and a super awesome boss since his grandmother passed away. I lick my lips and start my little speech. "I do, Mark—but I'm getting up there in age. I've done nothing with my life. I've gone nowhere. I have no education, no boyfriend, and no family." I sigh, again.

Mark lifts the fries from the grease, shakes them, and sets them aside. "You have a family, girl. What do you think we all are?" He nods his head. "We've been here the whole time. We aren't blind, we see you. If you need us, we're here for you. Always remember that."

Well, nothing like getting all sentimental." I sniff back the tears that want to fall. "You mushy fucker." I laugh. "Thank you." I go over to him and hug him while trying not to interrupt his awesome cooking.

Mark laughs. "Love you, baby girl. Grandma saw something in you long ago, and so did I. You're family through thick and thin. Always. Now get back to work." He puts the finishing touch on the burger he was working on. "Order up, bitch."

I laugh and take the plate from him. Looking at the slip I see it's for Jake. My laughter dies down as I walk away.

I'm a strong girl. I can do this. Jake's just a man—a damn fine looking man—but a man all the same. He's here to eat and then he will be gone. I got this.

With one foot in front of the other, I head in his direction with a small smile on my face. Setting his plate down, I ask him, "Would there be anything else?"

He just shakes his head no. Hmm, that's strange. He was more pleasant earlier. Maybe he noticed my hesitation...

"Well, I'm here if you need anything else." I tell him and walk away. I go stand at the bar and watch over everyone in the room. It's been a steady evening—which is good. It makes the time go by fast, but I dread the going home part. Going home alone. Alone to my thoughts. I really need to change things, spice things up. I need to plan what I'm going to with my life. That's what I'll do.

# CHAPTER THREE

*Jake*

Her smile changed. Body language stiff. The tone of her voice is a bit different from before. She probably doesn't realize the changes, but I think she realizes who I am and is freaked out. So much for her being my angel, my salvation, my redemption. She comes back with my food. I can tell she's trying to be nice, but I don't bother. I guess once a prisoner, always a prisoner. I keep my head down and accept the food. Nodding my thanks, I take the food and dig in.

Oh, my fuck. This burger is the best burger I've had in seven fucking years. Pun intended. I don't give a fuck that the grease runs down my chin or that I may have moaned while I chewed that first bite. It's fucking delicious. I dip some fries in the side mayo that came with and chew on them. Wow, they're amazing, too. Real food never tasted so good.

I lick my lips and wipe my face with a napkin. I don't want to look like a damn animal on my first night out. I glance around to see if anyone's looking. Nope, no one. Thank fuck. I chug back some Coke and dig back into the burger. Mmm. Yep, I did it again. I moaned from the deliciousness of the damn burger.

I finish the burger, there're just a few fries left. I sit back in the booth and let my food settle. I look around the modest diner and take everything in. There are couples, singles—people of all ages, young and old here. I'm surprised the place does such good business for a city this big. You'd think people would go to the fancy places, but what would I know? I'm just Jake Green, criminal.

21

I spot my blonde waitress across the way, her slender hips swaying as she walks mesmerizes me. Her laughter is the only thing I hear as I see her lean over and touch an older gentleman on the shoulder to pick up his plate. She may not be my angel, but she sure looks like one. Maybe I'm just not meant to be redeemed. I'll have to learn to crave something else in life. Only time will tell.

I watch her as she works the room. She cleans up like she has done it her whole life. From table to table, a smile here, a laugh there, she owns the room. I haven't seen any other waitress around, the only other server I have seen is the bartender. He hasn't come around the bar the whole time I've been here.

Blondie bends over to pick up a napkin that fell off a table close by, and the little black skirt she has on rides up a bit, flashing more skin. Of course my dick just has to twitch at that. Fuck. Her ass is perfect. Round and just, perfect for grabbing. Like a peach. I swallow deeply and continue watching. There's just something about her that grabs my attention. The mild ignorance she possessed earlier didn't last long. When I heard her first laugh, her magnetism tugged at me and I became a goner.

The girl's definitely quick on her feet. The next thing I know she stands beside me.

"All finished here?" She asks.

I look to her and smile. A genuine smile. "Yes, I sure am. It was delicious, thank you."

She looks taken aback for a second—but then a real smile appears. "You're very welcome." She set the check on the table and walks off.

That girl's confusing. I shake my head and pull my wallet out placing two tens on the table. It's more than enough to cover the bill and the rest will be for her. I wipe my face once more and get up to leave. Looking around the place, I think to myself that I'll be eating there frequently before I head out the door.

It's still semi-early since I slept all day, and I'm not really tired. I don't want to go and just sit in the motel, so I suppose I'll walk the streets for a bit. I have no place in mind to go to. Once outside the diner, I turn left and start to walk. Street lights are on, and people wander about in their drunken state. I notice a drug deal go down in a semi-lit alley, and grit my teeth at the thought that I once did that. I used to be that man. Geez, I used to be pathetic. I have so many wrongs to right.

The thing is people used to think I was this badass guy, when really I was just the side guy. Dominic—my other brother—was a hundred percent worse than me. Remember, five years my senior. Trained for more. Yeah. I wasn't innocent, but I didn't kill that man on purpose. I used to rough people up, sure. Sell drugs? Yeah, I did. Smuggle some guns? Unfortunately, I did. Whatever my pops ordered, I did. Why? Because I was a fucking idiot and was taught that I did what my father told me to. It was law in our house. If we didn't, we got our ass's handed to us.

I sort of think that's why I got out early. You see, my dad is really the bad guy and my brother is still at large. I cried like a baby at trial—because yeah, reality sunk in. Prison. For life. Fuck that. I was twenty-eight years old then, I had no education, no woman, and really no family. What did I really have to live for but myself? So I cried and spilled everything—well, not everything, but most. I told them about the abuse and how I was forced to do the things I did. I told them about the guy I killed, but didn't mean to. That I just thought I roughed him up, that he was breathing when I left him. But he'd gone and fucking died on me. I didn't give all details to my father's dealings because I knew I'd get out one day and fuck, I wouldn't want a hit put on me. So I only gave what I needed to. And I had to pay for my mistakes. Then there was the whole fuck up with Sean. My baby brother. My biggest regret.

I should've done everything in my power to keep him out of the life dear ol' dad forced on us, but I was too far gone, in too deep. I needed someone else to take his wrath. I couldn't take my father's beatings anymore. I needed someone to share the pain with me. I may have been an adult, but I still was under my father's thumb. Anyone living by his rules dies by them, too. Being beaten into submission on a daily basis became too much and I couldn't do it anymore. I was weak. Pathetic. It's a poor excuse, but that's all I have And then I went and turned on him. What a loser I was. When I think about it now, I don't even know why I did. Oh, wait—yes, I do. Because of my God-damn father. I hate that fucking man. I despise him. I hope he rots in hell.

I met with my parole officer before leaving the prison and I remember what he told me. One day at a time. It's a good thing to remember. That's how I'm going to have to live. One day at a time. Moment to moment—and maybe one day someone will forgive me, and some of the pain inside of me will leave. It's a heavy burden feeling like this, and I'd love to feel a lighter load one day.

I've been wandering the streets for a long time. When my mind is in overdrive, I lose focus of everything else around me. Damn. Stopping in my tracks I look around to see if anything is familiar. Across the street, I see a glimpse of blonde, just a short distance down, and I believe it's her. Just my luck. I smile to myself.

Should I go talk to her? I really want to—but I don't want to scare her off, either. Fuck, this shit is hard. I used to be so good at this. I used to be able to pick up chicks all the time. I was never nervous before.

A shadow jumps out at her and I hear her scream. I'm instantly on alert.

# CHAPTER FOUR

*Devon*

Emily (Mark's old lady) came in to close up tonight, and I get to leave early. It's a nice warm and breezy night, so instead of cabbing it as I would after a long busy night, I decide to walk. I put my headphones in and start the music on my phone. I cross the street from the diner and head in the direction of my place. I don't live too far, the street lights are all on, and if I walk the same route I walk during my day shifts, I'm good to go.

I'm a few blocks out when someone grabs me. It startles me and I scream. When my attacker pulls me around, I see someone with a mask on. He pulls on my bag and my headphones fall from my ears. "Oh, fuck this shit. No!" I pull on my bag. This fucker isn't getting my stuff. I've had enough shit tonight—it's not ending like this.

"Give me the bag, bitch." The masked man grunts.

I tug my arm and hit him with my free fist.

He pulls back and shoves me hard. I hit the ground with a thud—but I still have my bag. I take a kick to the ribs. I grimace and cry, letting go of my bag.

The man takes his chance, grabbing the bag and running.

"No…" I yell while holding my torso.

I hear footsteps running in my direction, and then the person runs right past me. To my surprise, it's Jake. What the hell is he doing here? I watch him run after my attacker. They both disappear around a corner. I'm still in shock over the whole thing, and try to shake my thoughts and assess the situation.

I hear footsteps come jog back and stop beside me. I look up. It's Jake, again. I still don't understand where he came from.

25

"Blondie, are you okay?" Concern is written all over his face.

Blondie, seriously? How original. I laugh a little, but it hurts. "What are you doing here?" I grumble.

Jake leans down to try and help me up. I don't want to be a complete bitch, so I accept his offer. I take his hand with one hand and cradle my side with the other.

"I was just walking when I heard a scream. Are you okay?" He pulls me to my feet with ease and holds me steady.

I go to step back from him and wince. I think the fucker cracked a rib or something when he kicked me. "Yeah, I'm just peachy." I pout, but in a bitchy way.

Jake snickers and shakes his head. "Where were you heading? Looks like the asshole got your purse." He puts his hands in his pockets and stands in front of me. "I tried to stop him, but he hopped a fence in the alley and I was concerned about you."

I dust the dirt off my skirt, adjust my shirt and look up at him. Damn, he's rather tall. Possibly six-foot-two or more, compared to my five-foot-five. "I was on my way home until that fucker jacked me…so, yeah—great ending to a wonderful night." I try to walk around him, but he stops me.

"Hey, let me help you home. You're injured." He states.

"No, Jake. It's okay, I'm fine. I just need… Shit!" I just said his name.

Jake steps back one step and looks down at me. "You know who I am?"

I blow out a breath and sigh. "Yes… I know who you are." Damn me and my stupid mouth. So much for being discrete.

Jake nods his head, I don't know if he was hurt or not, but his expression looks different than a minute ago. "Why didn't you say anything?"

Well, my night can't get any worse I suppose. I might as well be honest. "Because you scare me." I look down to the ground. I don't want to see the anger that he may direct my way.

26

Silence. I'm met with dead silence. He doesn't move, nor do I. After a minute I look up. He stares at me, a sad look on his face.

"I'd never hurt you, Blondie." He confesses, then turns and begins to walk away.

Did I seriously just hurt this man's feelings? He's the murderer and I, Devon, a simple waitress, hurt his feelings, you have got to be kidding me? Well fuck. Ugh.

"Wait up, Jake." I start after him, doing my best to ignore the pain in my ribs. "I'm sorry."

"What for?" He questions.

Huh, I've never been asked that before. He actually makes me think a minute. "Well, for starters, I hurt your feelings. Second, I wasn't overly friendly to you at Granny's." I grimace.

Jake raises his eyebrows and smirks. "Well, those are both true." His lips flatten out and he looks all serious now. "But I'm not a good man, Blondie. So you don't need to worry about hurting my feelings."

At least he's honest about himself. He isn't trying to disguise his past or possible present. Everyone deserves a second chance don't they? Or am I just a sucker, looking to get my heart broken or myself murdered? I hope I'm not wrong for what I'm about to do.

"Bad men have feelings too, Jake. Plus, everyone deserves a second chance." I look up at him and smile. I reach my hand out to him, hoping he accepts my gesture. "Walk me home, please. I don't trust that that fucker won't be back, I still have clothes that he could take." I laugh, again, it hurts, but I just cradle my side. Fear aside, Jake's still a person. I won't think of his past. I will think of now, just this moment. He is helping me, so only time will tell.

JEAN KELSO

# CHAPTER FIVE

*Jake*

Umm, what just happened here? This sure is a twist of events. She wants me to walk her home, even after I told her I was a bad person. She says everyone deserves a second chance, but do I? Well, I better not fuck this up. This sweet sassy and sexy-as-molasses little pixie just entrusted herself with me. She was just mugged and appears to be in pain. If I could have gotten there in time, I would've kicked that fucker's ass for laying a hand on her.

Time isn't on my side of course, but I at least get to escort her home to safety.

As we are walking toward her house, I notice that she trembles a bit. It's not cold out…she did say she was afraid of me, but I'm going out on a whim here and going to assume that it's from that she's in shock asshole terrifying her.

I gently wrap my arm around her for comfort. I hope I'm not overstepping, but I want her to know that she's safe at the moment. This is new territory for me, but it just seems right.

I look over to her to check for any sign of disgust or just plain fear, but I see nothing other than a small smile. I keep my arm there and we keep walking.

After a few minutes, I can't handle the silence anymore. "So, how do you know me?" I glance down and ask.

She peeks up once, twice and then speaks. "Oh, yeah, about that." Hesitation noted.

I notice her lick her luscious lips and contain the groan in my throat.

"I was in Sean's class all through school. And was friends with Jenn in high school, so…"

And she bites her damn lip. She's trying to kill me. I do believe she knows I just got out of jail. Fuck me stupid. I bet she doesn't even know she's doing it and that's the killer.

I look her over a little more. She doesn't look familiar at all. But then again, Sean was stuck like glue to Jenn all through school, so other girls didn't matter. "Yeah, I'm sorry. I don't recognize you."

"That's okay, I sort of kept to myself. When there was trouble, Sean helped out a bit, but that was all." She shrugs. "I wasn't really a loner per say, but I wasn't a partier either."

So little bro watched over another girl—and a friend of his girl. Hmm, I wonder if Jenn knew the extent of that relationship and the help he gave? Oh well, another story, another time. A big regret I need to fix.

"People change, that's for sure."

"I hope so." She whispers. I wonder if that was a dig at me or not. There's no way this fine woman was interested in me, was there?

There are a few more blocks of uncomfortable silence when she suddenly stops. We stand in front of a small blue house with a yard that needs some work. There are no lights on in the house, so no one's home.

"This is me." She whispers. "Thank you for walking me home."

I look to the house and back to her. "Looks like no one is home, are you able to get in?" I ask.

She repeats my actions and smiles. "Yes, I can get in. It's my house. I have a spare key hidden. Don't worry. I'm safe now. Thank you." She turns and heads toward the dark house.

"No problem, Blondie. Take care of yourself." Shit, I missed my chance. What am I saying, what chance? "By the way, you might want to change your locks since your keys were stolen. Better to be safe than sorry." The last thing I need is for her getting hurt after the fact. I turn and walk back in the direction I came. It's going to be a long walk back to the motel, but I think it's worth it after that.

I make it back to my motel room. It's close to midnight now. I'm still not overly tired, but I strip down to my underwear and sit comfy on the bed. I've had seven years of thinking about my life, about the mistakes I've made. I have tattoos and scars to prove the errors of my ways. The only thinking I need to do now is to figure out how to make up for those wrongs. To make right to all those who deserve the best. The top of the list I suppose should be me. I need to do what is right for myself. To fix what was done wrong to me. I need to salvage my identity and make it, to make me who I really want to be. And that isn't who I used to be. Too many years I did wrong. I can't do wrong anymore.

I find a pad and pencil in the drawer of the nightstand and I start to make a list. I have money in the bank, the judge said no one could touch it. They let me transfer my account to a tax free savings account of some sort. I was able to pay all my fines and the rest has been sitting there. I started saving money when I was a teenager before I became stupid and did as father directed me. There isn't much left after the fines, but it'll help get me a place to stay besides this dump of a motel, clothing and food in my stomach. Then I need to try and find a job. One thing at a time I guess. I'm starting over. I just hope nothing gets in my way and ruins it all for me.

**I wake early**, toss on the clothes I had on yesterday and head out. I grab a coffee to go from the vending machine and start walking. I try not to reminisce as I walk the streets of my home city, it's been years since I've been here, but it's hard to forget all the damages I've done. Being an enforcer for my father fucked with my head. Dad thought I killed people, but I didn't. Well— except the one, my one accident. Dad assumed them dead. After debts were partially paid (they needed some money to survive with) and they were nowhere to be found. The thing is, I'd kick ass and give them their one-way ticket out of the city. I'd tell them to run and never come back. I know beating the shit out of people was wrong, but the adrenaline I had from the fight was such a rush. After years of getting my ass handed to me by my father—not being able to defend myself until I was older—like seriously, if you could just understand. But I know now, it's wrong. My father was wrong. I've learned, just too late.

During my seven years in jail, I did a lot of soul-searching. I've had serious counseling and I actually made a good friend while on the inside. Jones was a man my dad's age and he had stories—man did he ever. He sort of took me under his wing during my time inside once I settled in and chose my path. When trouble came my way, he had my back and was certain to put a stop to it. Jones is a lifer, you see. He murdered his wife in a fit of rage, out of jealousy for stepping out on him. His biggest regret, but he's doing his time. He accepts his error in life. I guess if this man can accept fate—then I can, too.

After being beat down, tossed around and being told I was worthless during my childhood, I didn't want to disappoint my dad. I guess there was no making him happy—no matter what I did—and I only ended up hurting myself in the long run. I should've taken Sean when I turned eighteen and ran. But I didn't. I was stupid. I turned into my father, the last thing my mother wanted. Now I need to make my mother proud, bless her soul. I cleansed my sins when I confessed everything in court—well, almost everything. I gave up just enough about Connor Green and all his known associates like Simon, that it shouldn't hurt me in the long run. I explained to the judge, in private about how I helped get some of the people free of my father's wrath and gave some names so they could check into it. Thank Christ my leads panned out, and they did find those people alive out of state. They could testify that I did indeed help, but only after I hurt them. Fuck. See, regrets.

But hell—with what I gave to the judge, and prosecutor, they reduced my sentence from fifteen years to ten. My charges went from murder to involuntary manslaughter with a five thousand dollar fine. I got early parole for good behavior, and I just have to check in with my parole officer every now and again to make sure I'm keeping up with the rules of my release. I'd say it's a sweet deal considering the fucked up life I lived—or should I say suffered through. Now I know not everything was printed in the papers about what went down behind the closed doors between the judge and me, so people probably think of me the same as my father. I need to prove them wrong. I need to prove to myself that I'm not like him. Today's the start of my new life. I hope I don't fuck it up.

The first clothing store I find I head in. Not caring what the newest fashions are, I grab some tee shirts, underwear, socks, shoes, and a couple pairs of jeans. I pay and head out. One thing to check off my list.

# JEAN KELSO

# CHAPTER SIX

*Devon*

I normally love working the breakfast shift, but I didn't sleep worth shit last night. My purse is gone. I need to get everything replaced today and change my locks as Jake suggested. And then there's Jake. The feel of his arm wrapped around me yesterday left an odd tingle all over me through the night. I don't know if it was a good tingle or a bad one. I just know it was weird. I tossed and turned all night. Now I'm here at the diner, opening for breakfast at six in the damn morning. I'm exhausted and my emotions are a mess.

Granny's isn't a fancy diner, it's a casual place. It's meant to feel like home. We don't have uniforms, just name tags—but I don't wear mine. Mark gives me shit all the time for not wearing it. He says that the customers should know who their beautiful server is. I just roll my eyes at him and move on. We get a lot of regulars in here. Mostly everyone that comes in knows me. We do get a few stragglers, so I introduce myself most times. Last night, I didn't. It was busy and I was on a roll, so I didn't think of it and when I realized it was Jake—well, hell—I was definitely not giving names.

But today's a new day. I hope it goes by fast and nothing goes wrong. I had this really creepy feeling like someone was watching me this morning on my way to work. I don't know if it was the creep from last night, but I don't need any more trouble. I reach for the sugar jug from under the counter and head to the first booth. I need to get the place ready to open. The sooner I get shit done, the sooner I can go get other stuff done.

Wednesday mornings aren't generally that busy, maybe Mark will let me head out early after I tell him about last night.

Sugars filled, salt and pepper shakers topped off and napkins stacked. I'm just wiping down the counter when Mark walks in.

"Hey, baby girl! How was your night?" He asks.

I toss the rag into the little sink behind me and lean on the bar. "Sucked actually."

Mark hangs his jacket on the coat rack and turns to me. "How so?"

I blow a strand of loose hair from my eyes and sigh. "Well, for starters I was mugged on the way home."

"What the fuck, Devon? Why am I just hearing about this now?" Mark shouts. "After I tell you last night that you're family and that I'm here for you, you go through that and don't fucking tell me? Damn it, girl." He stomps through the door to the kitchen, the doors swinging back and forth vigorously.

I hear things clang around in the kitchen. Clenching my eyes tight, I blow out a breath and stand. "Mark!" I call out. He's mad. This was the last thing I wanted. I don't like making him angry.

Suddenly the doors whip open again and Mark comes stomping out again. "Jesus, baby girl. Are you at least okay?" He rushes over to me and pulls me into a bear type hug, running his hands down my arms like he is checking for injury. Uh, mood swings or what?

I wince when he squeezes because motherfucker my ribs hurt still.

"Fuck! You're not alright." Mark lets me go and sits on a bar stool and faces me.

I sit on a stool beside him and get ready to talk. I explain what happened—about how Jake came to my rescue even though it was late and how he escorted me home to safety. Mark still seemed angry, but was glad that I didn't end up in a body bag somewhere.

"So since I have no purse, I have no ID or anything. I need to leave as early as I can today. I need to get all new stuff." I give my best puppy dog eyes and smile I have. "I also need new locks because my keys were in my purse. So, would that be okay with you?" I request.

"Ah, baby girl. I'd do anything for you. You're like a little sister to me. I wish you realized that." Mark takes my hands in his and gives them a little squeeze. "We don't open for another half hour. Let me call the wife in so you can take today off to get your shit settled. Sound good?"

I stand carefully and lean in to him to hug him. I never realized how much Mark really meant to me until now. Hearing him talk like this—being a real man and not just a boss—kind of makes me emotional. And it's not even that time of the month, so I can't blame my hormones. I can feel my chest tighten from the emotions between us and fight it. I'm not going to cry right now. "Mark, you make an awesome brother." I smile big and step back and head to the coat rack for my purple sweater. "Thank you." I head out feeling lighter, better knowing that I have someone on my side.

I lost everything because I'm silly enough to carry all of my identification with me in my purse. It takes me all morning just to get proof of registration of my birth from the hospital. They tell me I need to get a new copy of my birth certificate, and driver's license. I've already called and canceled my credit cards, and now head to the bank to get a new debit card. The hairs on my neck stand up and an eerie feeling comes over me. Is someone following me? I stop and look around. Nothing out of the ordinary. Must just be my nerves. I continue on my mission.

With a temporary birth certificate, temporary driver's license and a new debit card, I head to the hardware store to grab new locks. My purse held my cell phone, money, and some makeup. A few random photos, but those I can always print off again from my memory stick.

I head to the cellular store to grab a new phone and sim card. I ask for a new number just to be sure. Picking out a pretty purple case, I pay and walk home to sort the rest of my life out.

Just as I walk inside, my stomach growls. I haven't eaten all day—too much on my mind. After setting the envelope of new documents and bag with new locks on the table, I set out to make a grilled cheese sandwich. That should tide me over for a little while.

Sitting down with my very cheesy sandwich and an ice cold glass of water, I suddenly hear a noise at the front door. My body tenses. Then a knock sounds.

I'm not expecting anyone, so I cautiously set my sandwich on my plate and head to the door. I gently lift the chain and hook it on. My heart beats a little faster than normal, so I take a calming breath. "Who is it?" I call out.

"It's Jake."

I take a step back from the door, confused. Why would he be here at my house? I slowly reach up and unchain the door. I hope I'm not making a mistake. He hasn't hurt me yet, so I hope he never does.

# CHAPTER SEVEN

*Jake*

I know I shouldn't be here, but there just seems to be a pull coming from her—a magnetism, if you will. I want to make sure she's okay...and I suppose selfishly, I just want to see her again.

I hold the small bouquet of flowers I picked up on the way over behind my back. My pulse pounds strongly in my chest. I'm so fucking nervous. My palms start to sweat. This woman will be my undoing.

I hear the chain move from the door and it slowly opens. Her beautiful face peers around the thick door as it moves and a slow smile shines.

"Hi, Jake."

I immediately pull the small bouquet of pink flowers from behind me and extend them to her. "These are for you." I stutter my words. Fuck really, I stutter? This is bad.

The look of surprise says it all. I read her completely wrong last night. Shit. I blow out a breath and look down, shuffling my feet. Then I hear her soft, angelic voice.

"They're gorgeous, thank you." I look up to see her beaming now—her smile so big with her teeth showing. "Would you like to come in?" She asks me.

"I'm not interrupting anything, am I?" I ask and tip my head slightly to the right.

She slowly shakes her head back and forth." Not at all. I was just having a sandwich. Please, come in." She steps aside and walks timidly (but quickly) toward a table.

I quickly step in and shut the door as I pass the threshold. I take a minute to glimpse around. Her home's small, but it suits her.

JEAN KELSO

Nice furniture, wall colors are decent, but fading, all in all, a pretty good place. "You have a nice place." I move at a normal pace toward her.

She seems to be finishing a mouthful as I see her rushing a chewing job. It's cute. "Thank you. Please, come sit." She motions with her hand to the dining chair across from her.

I pull out a small sized, brown wooden chair and sit at her small table and smile. "Go ahead and finish, I can wait." I grin.

She takes one more bite and sets the sandwich on the plate, chews and takes a drink. Wiping her mouth, she says. "I'm good, thank you. I can finish later. What brings you here today?" She looks up to me, her bright eyes staring into mine.

I get comfortable in my chair and continue to gaze into her stunning eyes. Such gorgeous eyes. They say you can see people's souls through their eyes. I don't know what I see, but I'm definitely drawn to her—in more ways than one. "I wanted to make sure you were okay from last night, and to see if you needed help getting stuff back. I also wanted to remedy the name thing." I smirk at her, drawing one side of my mouth up.

She sits back in her wooden chair, breaking eye contact by looking down to her lap. She seems nervous now. Avoiding my eyes and biting her cheek, by the looks of it. After a moment, she glances back up. "Devon. My name's Devon." She bites her lip again, appearing even more nervous, anxious. Chewing on her bottom lip, if she doesn't stop, I'm sure blood will start to leak from it.

Devon. Such a beautiful name. I look to her and smile huge. "A beautiful name for a beautiful woman." I watch her skin flush with heat. I do make her nervous. I'm not sure if that is good or bad. I guess only time will tell.

"Thank you." She stops chewing on her lip and whispers.

Her soft spoken words make my heart flutter. What the fuck? A massive pull to her, and now a flutter. Fuck, I'm in trouble. I have never had feelings like this before for a girl. So help me God,

I hope not to fuck it up. I want to be a better man. The last thing I want is for Devon to get hurt. Just because I'm out of prison, doesn't mean trouble won't come looking for me. Shit!

Instantly all my nerves are on fire. My skin tingles and I feel pins and needles all through my body. I don't know what I'm doing. I can't get Devon hurt. Fuck!

I jump up from my chair. Surprise cover's Devon's face instantly. "Can I use your bathroom?" I inquire.

"Just down the hallway, first door on your right." Her voice is full of concern, and her eyes narrow.

"Right." I hurry down the little hallway and shut the door behind me. Leaning my hands on the cool tiled vanity, hunching over, I start taking deep breaths. I need to calm my shit. Don't lose it now. You got this.

I turn the taps on and begin to splash water on my face. With the water and the breathing, my nerves finally start to settle. Pins and needles subside, and my skin starts to feel normal.

A knock on the door startles me. "Jake, are you okay?"

Of course I freaked Devon out—jumping up from the damn table and running off like a mad man. I turn the water off, wipe my hands and face off with a towel that hangs behind the door. Taking a final deep breath, I open the door.

"Yeah, Blondie. I'm good now. Sorry to scare you." I step out of the small bathroom as she steps back. "Let's go sit in your living room. I want to explain some things to you." I reach for her petite hand, but she pulls hers back. I sigh. Moving forward I go and sit on the cozy looking couch. I hope she sits beside me—and she does.

"I want—no, I need to explain some things to you. You may not want to have me coming around after I tell you, but I like you, Blondie. I know it is fast, but I can't help it, I feel what I feel....and I think you need to know. Sorry, Devon." I breathe deeply. "But I think you need to know." I face her and look her straight in the eyes.

JEAN KELSO

# CHAPTER EIGHT

*Devon*

I sit beside him on the couch. I haven't got a clue what he wants to explain, but I have a deep sinking feeling that I need to hear him out. The way he rushed away from the table—the hurt, the pain, and anger all were prevailing in his body language and facial expression—I didn't know what to do, but let him go. I've learned over the years to not let someone stew for too long. So I didn't, and now here we are. He said he likes me. As scary as it sounds, I feel this pull toward him, and I think I might like him, too. Strange as it is since we just met, but I'm willing to jump. He's definitely not the man I knew from school, but there's lots of time to get to know each other. Past or no past.

Jake looks troubled—like he has so much on his mind. I can't imagine what all he's been through. I suppose I'll do my part. Listen. I get comfy on the couch and face him. "Okay, Jake, hit me. What do you need to explain?" I return his stare and wait.

I watch Jake take a breath. His eyes close for a moment then open. Eye contact continues. His eyebrows scrunch up and he starts.

"I wasn't always a bad person. My father, Connor, made me into the man he wanted. He wanted an enforcer. A debt collector. So that's what I became." He pauses.

I reach for his hand that rests on his thigh and give it a squeeze. "Go ahead. I'm listening." If anything, I can be a good listener for him. He seems to really want to get it off his chest, so I hold my own thoughts and questions and take everything he says in.

"Fuck, this isn't easy." Jake grumbles. "Okay. So one thing people probably didn't notice over the years was that dad used to beat the ever-loving shit out of us on a daily basis. And when I say us, I mean Dom, me and Sean. He thought we were weak, and he wasn't going to have weak sons."

I can tell he struggles with sharing his story. My chest begins to tighten with each of his words. They were beaten as kids. I never knew. Sean never told me. Jenn never told me. Maybe Jenn never knew?

Jake squeezes my hand and continues. "Dad ran a few businesses and the majority of them were illegal. Drugs, guns, etc. I hated being his enforcer. Every time I had to go out for a job, dad would literally kick my ass and get me riled up so my anger was set." Jake let go of my hand and shot up from the couch.

"Fuck! Every person I hurt I pictured my father. Every blow to the face, head, ribs, I imagined I was beating him. But it was never him. When my vision cleared and I realized it wasn't him, just some dirtbag that owed my asshole of a father money, I shut down. I did what I could to get them safely out of the country. I had to make them disappear. Make my father think that they were dead." His voice trembled at the tail end and I felt so sad for this poor man. For what he went through, for what he has done.

"Nobody ever died by my hands. That's until the night my father killed my mother. The rage I felt. I carried it with me to the next job. I tried to contain it. It was an accident, I swear. On that final push—the surge of energy I had at the time, it was too much. When the guy fell and hit his head, he was still breathing. I gave my usual spiel to the wife about meeting up for new identities and left." Jake leans back on the couch and pulls on his hair while staring up at the ceiling. "But the motherfucker ended up dying. When he fell, he hit his temple and I guess I only saw what I wanted to see. He'd died instantly." Jake's breathing hard. He looks down at me and I can see the scattered tears running down his face. "It was a motherfucking accident, and it ruined me for life." He sniffs back his tears, stands and begins to pace. I guess he isn't done.

I sit back on the couch and just watch this poor damaged man spill his past to me. There's nothing to do but listen. Everything in me yells to go to him, to hold him…but he isn't done. There's more to be said. I can see it with how he contemplates his next words, so I wait. I watch as he paces and struggles with the words he wants to say.

Jake grunts and continues. "And then—to top it all off—I followed my dad's orders again and went against my own brother. My baby fucking brother. The one who should've been safe from all the shit, but I was too stupid and weak to keep him out of it." He shakes his head and paces some more. "I hurt his girl. I actually was going to hurt her really good. That's how fucked up my father had me. Then when Sean got them both away, dad's associate Simon and I actually chased them to Vegas. Fucking Vegas. Can you believe that? But the thing is, Simon had his own agenda and I didn't realize that. Simon was the type that was always out for blood. Simon was a killer. He took everything to the extreme. But this was my brother. I didn't want to hurt my brother. But he betrayed my dad. He turned on family for a girl. It hurt." The tears run down his face, he wasn't stopping them now. He paces his way to the couch again and sits down.

"I was so fucked up that I was actually going to kill my baby bro and his girl. My father told me, it was them or me. I wasn't trying to be selfish—but I wasn't ready to die, either." Jake's sad, tear streaked face turns to me. "It didn't help that dad sent Simon with me, so options were limited."

My heart felt like it was bleeding for his poor soul. I don't know what to do. He is broken. So emotionally broken from a bastard of a father. How can a parent do such a thing?

I position myself over him by straddling his lap, and reach my hands up to cup his cheek. I wipe some of the tears that run down and give him a sad smile. "It's not all your fault, Jake. Your dad's an evil child abuser. You did what he made you do. Brainwashed you, you could say. You're not that man anymore. Are you?" I ask him and lean into him, wrapping my arms around him and laying my head on his shoulder. I hold him. I want him to know that I'm here for him. That someone is willing. That I will listen and that I can take whatever he wants to dish out.

I can feel his chest shudder. He sniffles. Reaching up, he must wipe his face. "No, I'm not that man anymore. I want to be a good man. If I can, I want to make up for what I did in the past." He then wraps his arms around me and we just sit there.

# CHAPTER NINE

*Jake*

Pressure begins to lift off my shoulders. The more I tell Devon about the shit I've done and been through, the lighter I feel. Fuck, it feels good. I tell her everything, even about Sean. I feel somewhat free. It's like a weight has been lifted off my chest and I can breathe easier.

Sitting on the couch with Devon in my lap holding me, a new wave of perceptions come over me. I feel I can be redeemed. It's like a blessing of a different kind. It's a weird sensation, but it feels right. With her arms around me, I can smell her amazing flowery scent—and I feel calm. I wrap my arms around her and then suddenly, everything in the world seems better. At this moment, I'm free and the world's perfect.

There are no men out there that could be looking for me for giving my father up—well, that I know of. There's no bounty on my head for all the harm that I'd caused. No, at this particular moment, everything is right in the world. I can breathe. Maybe Devon is my angel. I was right all along. That would be a first.

Maybe with some time and with Devon's help, I'll try and seek forgiveness from Sean and Jennifer. Besides getting myself straightened out, that'll be one of my top goals for my future.

I've missed out on so much with Sean's life with being the horrible brother I was, and then being in jail, so out of touch. I did hear he and Jenn got married, but did they have a family? I hate myself for the life I led. I have so much to resolve. With the light I hold in my lap, I sure hope I can make a better future for myself with less remorse and maybe have something that resembles happiness.

Looking into Devon's eyes, I can sense some of what she feels. There's no fear there. At least at the moment. Understanding? Yes. Hope? Maybe. And then there's kindness and caring. As sassy as this petite woman is, her kind soul shines brightly. I'm not used to having kindness in my life. It's rare, but I like it.

I smile at her and give her a gentle squeeze. "Thank you." I whisper.

Devon scrunches her eyebrows. "What are you thanking me for?" She sounds confused.

"For listening. For not running. For just being you I suppose." I take a deep breath and wait.

Devon relaxes into me and smiles. "Oh, well you are most welcome."

We stare at each other. Time passes slowly. My thoughts begin to change as the minutes pass. Devon adjusts her legs and breathes deeply. I must affect her. I know she sure the fuck is affecting me. With her just sitting in my lap—knowing that her nice warm pussy is just hovering over my covered cock—is messing with my head. I clench my jaw and pray she doesn't feel that I'm hard as stone beneath my jeans. Devon's a sexy little angel and I haven't been laid in years. I don't want to take advantage of her—but fuck, just picturing my hard cock in her tight pussy makes the thought of taking advantage worth it. But I won't.

My breathing begins to get a bit heavy. I dig my fingers into her hips. My thoughts are beginning to take over.

"Jake, are you okay?" Devon asks me.

I shut my eyes trying to contain myself. I hear words. Then she touches me. Her skin is soft even though she only touches my face.

"Jake. You're scaring me. Are you okay?" Devon calls out as she attempts to leave my lap.

I grip her hips and contain myself. Blowing out a breath, I open my eyes and look at her. "I'm sorry, blondie." I want to be subtle, sort of give a hint of my problem. I glance down to my hard as rock cock and grimace and then look back to her. She looks down, stares for a moment, bites her lip and looks back at me. She's blushing.

"Oh. I understand." Devon whispers.

Realizing I still had a grip on her, I release it and set my hands on the couch beside me. I just got finished telling her that I wanted to be a new man, I can't start off with screwing her brains out like she's just some whore to release the tension that's been built up for seven years. Fuck. I give my head a shake. "I'm sorry." I tell her. "Maybe I should go."

Devon moves herself to sit on the couch again and puts her hands in her lap. "You don't have to." She tells me, sounding sad.

I'm a fucking mess right now. I'm spilling the beans to sexy strangers that I want to fuck, but who I also don't want to hurt because I want to be a new man. See what I mean. I am a mess. "Devon, it's not you. You're fucking amazing. You don't know me from a fucking hole in the ground. You actually thought I was a murderer and here you let me in your home and listen to me ramble and watch me lose my shit." I blow out a much needed breath. "Seriously. It's me. I don't want to hurt you. I don't want to fuck this up—whatever you and I have started here. I want this. Friendship, whatever. I want it. Please just give me time." I stood from the couch, watching her sweet face the whole time. I lean down and place a kiss on her forehead. "Thank you. I hope to see you soon." I tell her and find my way out.

I hate leaving her like this, but I need to get out of here.

It's still early. I have no plans for the rest of the day. I should eat I suppose...maybe I'll stop at the store and grab some stuff to bring back to the hotel. As I'm walking, my thoughts go back to her house—to her, to her sitting on my lap, to her pussy. And I'm hard again. Fuck. I start walking fast. I think I'll just head to the hotel and have a cold shower.

I'm about a block from the hotel when I hear my name being called.

"Jake Green, is that you?" A man with a harsh voice calls.

I stop and look in the direction I hear the voice come from. Leaning against a store front wall is a tall, lanky man. He has long dirty hair pulled back in a ponytail and has tattoos on his neck. He doesn't look familiar to me, but he sure seems to know me.

"Yeah, I'm Jake—who the fuck are you?" I snarl. I need to have my back up. I don't know the guy and I'm sure my family has some enemies out here since the business went down.

The man stood from the wall and comes toward me. His hands in his pockets and boots untied. "Jake—man, it's me, Snake."

Snake? Who the fuck is Snake? "Sorry, man. I don't know anyone named Snake." I turn on my feet and start to leave.

A hand grabs my shoulder. "Are you fucking serious man? Jake. I'm Pike's brother. How can you not remember us? We run with your brother Dominic. Well, we did."

The guy is beginning to sound irritable. But who the fuck is Pike? I don't know either of the names. And I can definitely say my hard on is long gone now.

"Listen, Snake. I don't wanna sound like a prick right now—but I don't know any person named Pike and I don't know you. Sure Dominic is my brother, but you must have me confused with someone else. I'm sorry." I begin to stride away, hoping the guy got the hint.

My back gets stiff as the guy talks. "Okay. Yeah, I get it, man. Prison makes you forget shit. We might've been little people to you back then, but we were a big person's little people." He chuckles. "Dom was a big man and his followers sure miss having him around." I look back and watch the fucker walk away himself.

Well, fuck me. This little fucker was one of Dominic's lackeys. And if they think it's a big deal I'm out, what will Dom think? I said some not so nice things in court about him, but not enough to cause too much trouble for him. Fuck. But then again, if he really hated me, you would think he would have found a way to end me by now. He once told me blood was thicker than water, maybe he lives by motto…

I reach the hotel, put the key in the lock and let myself in. Slamming the door, I walk over to the bed and sit down. I rub my aching temples as a headache is kicking in. I really hope a shit storm doesn't come to town. I really want this life to work out. I fall back on the bed and yell. "Fuck!"

# JEAN KELSO

# CHAPTER TEN

*Devon*

Never have I had a man lay his soul bare to me and then walk out on me because he was turned on. What the hell is wrong with mankind? Sure we are complete strangers to each other, but I listened and took in everything the man said. I felt his pain and I want to help him. I literally want to kill his bastard of a father for doing what he did to his family. All that abuse, makes me sick for the kids that they were. And holy hell, the sexual tension between us—you could've cut it with a knife. I didn't want to take advantage of him after he bared his soul, but he is sexy as hell and was hard as a rock. I could tell he wanted it, I don't understand why he didn't jump the gun. Then again maybe he used to be that kind of guy and he said he wanted to change. Ugh, how stupid am I?

And now here I am, frazzled. I really need to do something about that.

I get up from the table and head to the bathroom. A nice hot bubble bath should be relaxing enough. I need to unwind from the day and the events from last night. I put the plug in the tub and turn the water on. I turn and grab the bath oils I want and proceed to put them in. I close my eyes and smell the flowery scent as the bubbles begin to rise. Perfect. I strip myself naked and step into the nice hot water.

I ease myself down deep into the hot steamy bath. The water settles against me as I lean back and take a nice soothing breath. I close my eyes and instantly I picture him. Jake. His eyes. His muscular body. A shiver runs up my spine with memories of his hard cock that was within my reach. The sexual heat that passed between us as I sat on his lap, wishing he would've taken what I was offering. All the previous fear I had of him, about his past, gone. Now in my mind, all I see is a man. A sexy broken man available for the taking.

Butterflies fluttered in my stomach. I blow out a breath and bring my hands up to my breasts. My nipples are hard and my pulse increases. Squeezing one breast, I slowly slide my other hand down my belly and to my throbbing pussy.

Sliding my fingers between my lips, I graze my clit and shiver with the intense feeling of pleasure. A tingling sensation flows up my spine, which encourages me to keep going. Breathing deeper, I push a finger in and feel myself clamp down. Inserting a second finger, I begin to slowly pump them in and out. Such an incredible feeling runs from my toes up to my stomach and I begin to moan—licking my lips as I begin to pant. Faster and faster my fingers move. I use my thumb to rub my clit and my body begins to gently spasm. I can't believe I've never done this to myself before. Closing my eyes, I picture Jake—imagine that it's his hand between my legs and my hips buck. With my other hand I pinch a nipple, gasping. These intense feelings begin, and I want to scream because it feels so good. Faster and faster I go—breathing harder, deeper. I fuck my fingers, pumping and grinding. Water splashes out of the tub. I can't control the sensations I feel. Overwhelmed with pleasure, I can't help it. I bite my lip just as I feel my orgasm hit and scream. "Jake!"

Blowing out a breath and relaxing back in the water, I feel like putty. I really needed that. I sure hope the next time I see Jake I don't feel so sexually charged.

Feeling so relaxed and sleepy after such an intense orgasm, I finish with my bath, get out and get ready for bed. I hope a good night's rest will relieve the rest of the stress and tomorrow will give me a better perspective on things. I need to try and figure out what Jake wants from me. And I need to figure out what I really want from Jake. He seems like he wants a fresh start, but can I really trust him? So far, I think I can. People can change, right?

I wake bright and early, not having to work until noon, but still feeling good and refreshed. I make quick on changing the locks which I should've done yesterday, but got sidetracked—better late than never, right? I make some coffee and read some of the book I've been reading on my kindle. I have this thing for Indie Authors, right now I am reading this super awesome sci-fi, romantic type book called Blood of Eve. It's the second book in the series and I just love it. The author has such a way with words and her characters are awesome. Plus, I'll never turn down a super-hot sex scene.

I'm in the middle of a scene in the book with my favorite character when my cell alerts me of a message. I've had this phone for less than two days, and I haven't been able to give it a lot of people so curiosity peaks. I reach over to the coffee table to pick it up and see the message.

**How are you this morning, blondie? Sorry for running out on you last night, can we met up and talk?**

Jake? When did Jake get my number? He must have high jacked my phone when I wasn't looking. Silly man, he could have just asked.

I instantly blush thinking back to last night, and screaming his name when I orgasmed. I suppose I can at least hear him out.

**I work at noon until close, but you can come into the diner and we can talk there if it isn't busy.**

I return his text and turn back to my book. I'm not even a full paragraph in and my phone alerts me again.

**I'll see you there, thank you.**

He's so polite. It's so hard to picture him as the polite kind of man when you know he just got out of prison, but here it is, right in front of me. I push the shock of it aside, and keep reading. I try not to let the curiosity of what he has to say bother me. I know I'll learn of it soon enough.

Finishing my coffee, I look at the clock. It's almost time to head to work. Time has flown by while I read. I rinse my mug and go get changed for work. Styling my hair with little barrettes, and a light layer of make-up, I toss my phone in my new purse and head out. I hope this shift goes by smoothly. Now that the time has come, I'm nervous to hear what Jake has to say.

I arrive at work ten minutes early and see that the morning regulars have already left. There are only two customers sitting at the counter drinking coffee. It must've been a slow morning. I hope the day picks up, if it doesn't the day will drag on.

I hear the music playing in the kitchen, Mark's voice is harmonizing along with the tune. Such a great voice he has. Why he never did anything with it, I will never know. I head to the kitchen to see what he's doing and walk into a frenzy of bake goods.

"What the hell are you doing, Mark?" I laugh.

The singing stops and Mark turns to me in shock. He sets down the spatula that he has in his hand and grins. "I'm in the mood to bake. And with the diner being slow this morning, I thought I'd bake some cookies." Mark winks at me. "Wanna try one of my grandma's famous peanut butter chocolate chips?" He hands me a cookie and I take it.

I bite into the cookie and moan. Damn, that's one good cookie. "Holy shit, Mark! This is good." I'm in shock. I know Mark can cook, but Emily usually does the desserts around here.

"And to think just this morning Emily said I was good for nothing. That woman knows nothing." He laughs. "I showed her, right?" He laughs again then turns back to the stove.

I shake my head and leave the kitchen. I don't want to leave the customers alone since as soon as I walked in, Emily ran out mumbling something about being late for something.

A few lunch customers come in while I'm filling sugar containers. Two men who look they have seen better days walk by me. I wipe my hands on a towel and head to the table they sit at.

# JAKE'S REDEMPTION

"Hey, boys. What can I get you today?" I ask them as pleasantly as I can and wait with a smile. I notice the tattoos that they both sport and wonder if they hurt. I shake the thought from my head.

"Two orders of chili fries', sweet pea—and two cokes, too." The one guy on my left speaks up. He has a ring in his lip and the look he is giving me is giving me the willies. I write that down on my notepad and smile.

"Coming right up." I turn and start toward the kitchen. As I walk away I can hear him mumbling. I hear something about a sweet ass and cringe.

I give my order to Mark and get the drinks ready. Grabbing a couple straws, I bring the drinks back to the boys and set them down. "Your order will be just a few minutes."

Both guys glare at me with wild looks. I'm not sure what to think, but the feeling I get isn't good. Are they on drugs? I just don't know. I walk away and hear the bell go off at the door. I turn to see who it is, and there he is. Jake. My breath catches. I don't know why, but just seeing him makes me feel better. I smile at him and head back to the kitchen.

# JEAN KELSO

# CHAPTER ELEVEN

*Jake*

After such a rough night I can't wait to see Devon's ray of sun shine brightly this morning. All I could think about last night was her tight body on top of mine, every curve sitting right in front of me waiting for me to touch it, to take it and I just couldn't do it. As much as it pained me, I just couldn't do it. At least not yet. I need to learn restraint. Earn her trust. And man if last night wasn't a lesson, I don't know what is.

I woke in the night horny as all hell from an erotic dream of her. I dreamt that I had her tied to my bed, blindfolded and I was thrusting the shit out her from behind and she was screaming with so much pleasure that I woke with such a hard on that I just couldn't ignore. I had to jack off twice to get any relief. Never in my life had I had a dream like that.

Such an innocent woman, so beautiful and sweet...and I'm going to taint the fuck out of her.

No, that was the old Jake, I'm not that man anymore. I can do this. I'm strong enough.

I texted her this morning tell her I wanted to talk to her. I need to explain myself. I need to let her know that the ex-convict got fucking scared. That'll go over well, won't it? Oh, well. I don't want to do anything to hurt her, so I fled. I hope she understands.

I walk into the diner and am instantly greeted with her bright smile. I'm put at ease. Smiling back, I head to a booth and sit down. I quickly glance around. The place isn't too busy so that is good. We'll get a chance to talk...well, hopefully.

I sit back in the booth and watch her work. She looks amazing in her jeans and tight fitting tee shirt today. Her hair is pulled back just enough to reveal her beautiful bright eyes. Watching her hips sway is making me think of what I could do to her when I get a hold of those sassy hips. My cock twitches and I groan under my breath. Fuck, she's just working and I'm getting hard already. What the hell is wrong with me? I came to talk to her, not fuck her.

I look to see where she's heading with the food and see the same guy from last night. The hair on my neck begins to stand up. What the hell's that guy doing here? And who the fuck's with him? Calm down Jake, you need to relax. He was in the neighborhood last night, so he must be from around here.

Devon sets the food down and walks over to me. "Hey. Can I get you anything?"

I push off my tense mood and smile up at her. "Sure—just a coffee for now, thanks." She nods at me and walks off. I glance back over at the guys and see that they are looking at me. Or were they watching Devon? Fuck. I don't know what to think.

Looking away, I frown to myself. I can't let those guys get to me. I'll keep a close eye on Devon just in case.

I shake my irritability off just as Devon comes back with my coffee. She sets it down along with some creamer. "Thanks."

"No problem."

She's about to leave when I reach for her wrist. She stops and looks at me. She appears nervous and that is upsetting to me. She has no reason to be nervous.

"Do you have time to sit?" I look around the diner. It's not busy at all. There are only two other tables besides me and we all have been served. "Please?" I ask. I remove my hand from her wrist and set it on the table. I don't want to force her to do anything she's not ready for. Even if it's just talking. I open a creamer and put it in my drink and stir it.

After a few short moments, she finally answers. "Yes, I can sit for a few minutes." I notice her look around the place, wipe her hands on her pants then move into the booth, setting her hands in her lap. "What do you want to talk about?" She licks her lips, making them damp with moisture.

I take a sip of my coffee and take a quick minute to collect my thoughts. I need to choose my words so she doesn't think that I'm the asshole I used to be. "I want to explain my reasons for what happened last night."

Devon immediately pipes up, reaching across the table for my hand. "No, it's okay, Jake. No explanation's needed."

I take her hand in mine and give it a gentle squeeze. "Yes, Devon there is." I take my hand back and sip my coffee once more. Fuck, I'm nervous admitting this. I look into her eyes—wanting her to see me, to hear me. "I was scared. Like seriously, bat shit crazy scared. I was afraid I'd hurt you last night and that's the last thing I want to do to you. I know very little about you, but I want to know you. Hurting you isn't an option for me."

I notice Devon's eyes glisten and her lips begin to tremble. "Oh, Jake. You wouldn't have hurt me. I opened myself to you, for you. I wanted you..." Devon wipes the tear that starts to run down her cheek. "Christ, I wanted you to touch me so much that when you up and left, I thought I did something wrong." She looked down at the table and began to fiddle with her hands. A nervous habit, if I ever saw one.

She thought she did something wrong? Jesus. Does she really not know anything about my past? She said she did, and any normal person would be scared of me. Fuck. "Oh, Devon, I wanted to touch you. Believe me. The things you make me feel—what it makes me want to do to you. I wanted to strip you bare right there on your couch. But my emotions, all the anger I've built up from my past, I don't want it to get in the way. I don't want it to interfere with..." Devon's cheeks flush as she looks around to avoid looking directly at me.

"Miss, can we get our check please?" The guys across the diner call out. Go fucking figure we would get interrupted. Devon looks up at me, then over to the customers.

"Be right there." She tells them. "Can we finish this later?"
She asks me.

I blow out a deep seated breath. I was on such a roll with my so called speech, I don't know if I will be able to get it out again. But I'll do anything for her. It's happened fast, but I'm hooked. "Yeah, anything for you, Devon." I smile at her then look at the guys across the way. I'm getting a weird feeling that something isn't right with them being here. But then again, coincidences do happen. Yeah right, and the stares they are giving are a figment of my imagination. Something definitely is up. I finish my coffee, put some cash on the table and leave just a minute or two after the men. What's the name of the one guy? Snake. Yeah, that's it. He was talking about some guy named Pike. Maybe that is who the other fucker is. Either way, I don't trust them.

I head out of the diner and attempt to follow them. But they are already gone. Shit. Well, I will just have to be here to walk Devon home after her shift. If I remember correctly, she said she was closing tonight. I check the sign on the door for dates and hours of opening and the closing times and memorize it. With my mind made up, I head back to my hotel.

# CHAPTER TWELVE

*Devon*

He was scared. He wanted me. How can a man of his caliber be scared of me? I watch him leave the diner as I wipe the table clean. I need to get to the bottom of this so-called fear of his. Did he think he would hurt me physically? Now that I know the attraction between us is felt by both of us, I want answers. There has to be more to his past than he lets on. What is there that I don't know?

The rest of my shift goes by steadily until about an hour before closing. Emily calls and asks Mark to stop at the drugstore to pick up some medicine since she isn't feeling well. Mark decides since things are slow, he'll leave me to close up.

I tell him to wish Emily well and lock up the back doors. After shutting down the big fryers, I begin to clean and sanitize the counters.

Not once has the bell gone off at the front door. The kitchen's clean and it's time to finish up front. I head out there and turn the coffee machines off. I lean on the counter with my head in my hands. My imagination begins to wander. What could possibly be holding Jake back? I have never had such an attraction before to a man, and so soon. The so-called little crush I had for him in school was just that, a teenage crush. What I feel now..well, I can't really explain. It's not love that I know. I don't know him enough to say its love. Nor have I known him long enough, but I can picture a future if the connection stays strong.

Turning the lights off, I grab the diner key from my purse and head out the door. With the key in the lock, something startles me.

"Hey." I hear from behind me. I jump.

Dropping my purse, I turn around. It's Jake. "Jesus fuck, Jake. You scared the shit out of me." I turn toward him and smack his chest.

Jake chuckles and apologizes as he moves to pick up my purse.

"Here—sorry about that. I thought you saw me through the door." He hands me my purse with a slight smirk on his face. Oh, that devil of a man. Even after scaring me, he still makes my heart pitter pat for other reasons.

I take my purse, turn and finish locking the door. "Thank you. And no, I didn't see you. It's dark out, you know." I turn back and glare, trying to look stern, but obviously not doing a good job because Jake's smiling.

I let my little act drop and I return his smile. Tossing my purse strap over my shoulder I ask, "So, what do I owe this pleasure of you being here?" I tip my head in question.

"I just wanted to walk you home, is all. Would that be okay with you?"

Well, isn't that sweet. Not stalkerish at all. I giggle internally. "That'd be great. Thank you." I tell him and begin to walk.

We get to my house and stand in front of my door. Reaching in my purse, I pull out my key and put it in the lock.

"I should get going." Jake says.

"If you feel you need to, sure. I'll be okay. The locks are changed." I lean into him to give him a quick hug. "Thank you." I mumble. I hope I'm not being too forward. I just want to express my thanks for his kindness. But Jake doesn't release me. He holds me by my arms and stares down at me.

"You are so beautiful. Do you know that?" His eyes ablaze.

I'm stunned. I wasn't expecting that. I bite my lip and shake my head no. Lost for words I stare back at him.

"I don't deserve you, but I'll be damned if I don't want you. I want you so bad it hurts." Jake leans closer to me and then his lips are on mine. Holy shit are they ever on me. Warm and controlling.

He nips at my lips and I can feel his tongue, eager for entrance. I open and let him in.

He seeks me out, I find him. He tastes my flavor, I taste his. Our tongues battle for control, thrashing around, lips crushing—no winner in this intimate event. It's a give and take situation.

Tingles of heat spread through me as Jake's hands begin to move freely about my body. He pushes me up against my door and instinctively my hands wrap around his neck. I let the moment take me. I can feel the tense muscles of his neck, and the want and need he expresses in his kiss. I feel it all. Battle of the sexes. I want it, too. But not out here. Not out in the open.

"Jake." I whisper between his lips. "We have to stop." And instantly his mouth's gone. His touch is gone. Jake steps back and he is breathing heavily.

With his eyes dark, and lips wet and swollen, he looks to me. "I'm sorry. I didn't mean for that to happen. Shit!" He curses.

No, I don't want him to think I don't want this. I do. Boy, do I want it. I press my finger on his lips shushing him. "Stop. You have nothing to be sorry for." I lick my lips, turn and unlock the door. Pushing the door open I look back at him. "Please, come in." I blush, and can feel the heat rising up my neck and to my cheeks.

He seems to hesitate, but not for long as I reach for his hand, tangle our fingers together as one and pull him in with me.

Once inside I wink and grin at Jake. I want him to know what I want. What I need. If the hints that I have been giving aren't enough, then I suppose I'll have to take the lead—but I hope he takes control.

I walk us further in and let go of Jake. Heading into the living room, I set my purse on the table. The door slams and I jump. Looking back at Jake, I realize he understood my hints and the hunger in his eyes means business. It looks like Jake's going to let his inner animal out to play, and I look forward to the game that he's going to initiate.

He stalks toward me, slowly. The glint in his eyes shines brightly and his hunger is extremely evident. A shiver runs up my spine as I stand there, anticipating his next move—his every move.

He stops right in front of me. Heat pours off of him in waves. "You just started a fire, blondie. I hope you plan to put it out." His eyes narrow and lids hood. A look of blazing, perfectly fitting to a description from a book I once read. It's hot. "You know that playing with fire gets you burned, Devon? But the only kind of burning you'll feel is the best kind."

Instantly, I'm off my feet and hanging over his shoulder. Shocked—but excited—I squeal. "Jake, what are you doing?"

With a smack on my ass, he starts walking with determination down my short hallway to my bedroom. "The fire needs stoking baby. And you are gonna help."

My breath catches and I bite with lip glee. I just dreamt about this last night and now it's happening!

His hand rubs up and down my leg as he walks into my room. Another slap on my ass, and it stings. But the sting feels good. Suddenly I'm in the air and land softly on my bed. Exhilaration flows through me. My heart beats faster and it's so hard not to smile. I look up at him. He stands at the end of the bed. A whole new man stands there. Not the broken man I've been getting to know, but an animal…a sexual being, out to please me and my every need. It's a whole different side of Jake and I like it. I like it a lot.

# CHAPTER THIRTEEN

*Jake*

It's like something snapped inside of me. A wink and a little sexy smirk, and snap. The caged animal inside, broke free. I needed to have her. To touch every part of her beautiful body. To claim her soul and make her mine. This act is pure selfishness. Pure pleasure. I'll have her screaming my name as I ram my hard cock into her wet, warm pussy and she'll never forget who she had between her legs last. She'll be mine. Mine to take as I please. I'll make amends with my sins another day. Today I free my inner animal. I'll have to see what comes tomorrow.

I stare down at Devon, watching her chest rise and fall in anticipation. A growl erupts from deep inside of me, and my heart pounds as my cock presses at the seams of my jeans, wanting to escape. The hunger I feel, I receive tenfold in return from her. Her eyes shine and her lips quiver. Pulling her down the bed, I lean down over her and begin to undo her jeans. Slowly. Teasingly. Staring at her wanton expression. She expels patience. Something I seem to be lacking, but am trying my damndest to express.

The zipper's down. I start to pull her jeans down. Red. I see red, thin panties. No, wait. I pull further. Fuck me, it's a thong. I close my eyes tight, take a slow, deep breath and try to calm myself. But I can't. I need her. I need her now. I can't wait. I rip the jeans off of her so fast, I hear her gasp.

Smirking, I lean up and pull my shirt up and off. My muscles flex and tense from the movements. My body knows what's going to happen. What it's going to receive. It may have been years, but it knows what's coming. Release. I'm quick with my pants as Devon's rapid breathing edges me on. She wants me, too. Her hooded eyes. Her hot skin. All the basic subtle hints. She knew what she was getting into. Now it begins.

I crawl up onto the bed with her—moving over top of her. Caging her in. Grinning. I dip down and press my mouth to hers. Her lips are warm and inviting, opening for me without question. My desire spikes.

She gives as good as she gets, nipping at my lips with her teeth. Arching her body up and pressing her chest to mine. Devon's as hot as I am for this. Primed and ready. Caressing my hand up her stomach, I swipe the side of her breast. Hearing her moan is my undoing. I lean back instantly. "Arms." I demand and reach for her shirt. I want it gone. I need skin on skin. I want to feel all of her. I pull her shirt off in one fell swoop and a red lacey bra now tortures me. My throat feels dry, but it won't stay that way for long. With a deep swallow, I'm better.

Leaning down, I nip at each breast as I reach around and undo the clasp. Slowly I slide down the straps, and toss the bra aside. I stop for a moment and stare. "Beautiful. Just perfect. More than I could have imagined."

Devon blushes and I dive back in. I can feel her body tremble. Licking her neck, her jaw, her lips, I use my legs and nudge her legs apart to make room for me.

She spreads easily and I move in. Her warmth calls for me. Her moans are like a siren whispering my name. I kiss her deeply and rub my hard cock against her. Wet, warm and inviting. I grind my teeth to hold myself back. I want to ram myself balls deep inside of her right now, but I know I need to slow down. It can't be just about me. I have to think of Devon, too.

"Shit, Devon. You're so wet."

"Jake." Devon groans.

"Condoms." The word pops in my head instantly. I need to be safe. Safe for both of us. And kids aren't an option right now. I don't need to bring a baby into my life when I am just starting anew.

With a shutter Devon slurs. "Nightstand drawer." Her lips glisten from our kisses.

I ease back and lean over to the stand—nearly ripping the drawer out. Digging around, I find a box. Condoms. Thank fuck. I dump the box on the bed and take a wrapper. I look down at Devon and smirk. A sexy glint shines back.

She takes the wrapper from me, rips it open with her teeth, and slides it on my rigid cock. Oh, my fucking God! I'd never experienced that before and it's fucking HOT.

With the condom on, I eye Devon again. Her chest heaves, but her breath is steady. Need is evident in her eyes—and I plan to relieve the tension.

Slowly I caress my hand up her leg to hip. From hip to her chest, my fingers lightly touching her heated skin. She moans to my every trace. Leaning down again, I crush my lips to hers. I thrust my tongue in her mouth like a savage, a wanton man in need of her very soul. She accepts me, and her tongue fights me back.

Sliding my hand into her hair, I grip a hunk of it and gain control. Centering my cock to her pussy, I can feel the heat radiating off of her. I rub once, twice, and press forward. Inch by inch I move in, it feels like fucking heaven. I feel Devon's nails dig into my skin the deeper I go. I swallow every moan she gives.

"Jake. Oh, Jake." She moans over and over.

Fully seated inside, pressed hard at her pelvis, I hold still. Grounded. I nibble her bottom lip and look into her eyes. "You feel so fucking incredible, Devon." I smile and lick my lips. Grinding my hips around, I can feel her clench her pussy on my cock. I feel as if I'll go cross-eyed with pleasure. Heck, I could possibly bite my damn tongue off—it feels that good. I've been a starving man and this proves it.

Devon runs her hands up and down my back. Her legs spread further then lift and wrap around my waist. Licking her lips once again, she smirks. "I'm glad I can be something. Now, are you going to stoke the fire or what? Because you're killing me here."

The glint in her eyes shows that she teases, but I can also tell that she wants what I'm holding back. And I am holding back. I don't want it to end too quickly, and if she keeps squeezing me like she is, I might lose my load before I get the chance to please her. With her eagerness, it's as if she has been waiting a long time for what I am giving. Possibly, as long as I have.

I pull back and thrust hard. A tingle soars up my spine. Oh, my God—that feels so fucking good. I do it again, just a little harder, and Devon moans. Her legs squeeze around me and her nails dig in.

She wants the fire stoked, then I'll stoke it for her. I pull back and let my animal loose, thrusting fiercely in and out of her. I fear I may break her headboard, but hearing her breath, short and raspy, is heightening my excitement and making me want to give her more. I feel her pussy grasping me in such a merciful way that the pleasure is indescribable. I don't want it to end. I reach around and grab her ass cheek. Squeezing it once, slapping it and pulling her closer. I'm able to get deeper and am hitting something new. Her whole body starts to tremble. She looks incredible.

"Don't stop. Fuck. Don't stop." Devon whispers sexily. Her breathing increases as her eyes clench shut. "Fuck. Fuck. Ahh…Jake. More. Keep going."

Well, fuck me, talk about an ego builder. Leaning down I suck a nipple into my mouth and suck hard as I pump constantly in and out of her. A tingle begins at the base of my spine and I know I won't be long. I let her nipple go with a pop and repeat with the other.

"Jesus fuck, Devon. I'm gonna blow. Are you…" Her pussy clenches and starts to spasm.

"Jake…" Devon screams as her whole body tensely shakes and then spasms as she starts to orgasm. I keep thrusting, but watch as Devon looks like a fucking goddess, glowing as she cums.

JAKE'S REDEMPTION

A final thrust and my body tenses. "Fuck, Devon." I shout. My release starts and finishes just as Devon finishes. Damn. Talk about pent up sexual tension. That was exhilarating.

Spent. I'm done. Well, at least for the moment. I slowly pull out and roll to the side after Devon releases her grasp on my body. We lay there naked in her bed, both of us breathing heavily, but sated.

JEAN KELSO

# CHAPTER FOURTEEN

*Devon*

Lying in bed curled up with Jake, I think to myself how fast and how far I've come. To think I feared this man in the beginning all because of the news! The news didn't have all the facts. I got the truth from the source and a lot of what was reported was lies and a whole lot of rumors. Sure, Jake wasn't completely innocent, but he did his best in the circumstances of the life he was provided. He sought intervention and now he is trying to make amends. Everyone deserves a second chance. I want to be his chance. His redemption in the hell he was given.

I can hear his heart beat as my head rests on his chest, strong and steady. His breathing is slow and calm. I reach my hand up and run my fingers down his naked chest, down to his belly button. I peer up at him and notice a small smile form.

"How are you feeling?" Jake asks. His voice is sleepy, but I sense happiness in the tone.

Moving my hand up and under my cheek, I return the smile. "I feel great, actually. Better than I have in a very long time."

Jakes' arms wrap around me and he shifts his body so he's slightly on his side. One of his hands moves up and begins to brush my hair out of my face. "You look beautiful when you first wake up." He smirks. "Actually, you look beautiful all the time—and you look hot as fuck when you orgasm."

Heat begins to rise up my neck to my face. Embarrassment at its best. "Jake!" I scold. Slapping his arm, I close my eyes and pray he isn't laughing at me.

"Open your eyes, blondie. You don't need to be shy with me. I'm just telling you the truth."

I slowly open my eyes and see Jake look at me—no smirk, not laughing, nothing. He looks truly sincere.

"Okay." I whisper. "Sorry about that. I've just never had anyone be that honest before, nor have I been described as such. You just threw me off, is all."

Jake tips my chin up so I look right at him. "I want to be honest with you at all times, Devon. I want this. You. I want this with you. And for it to work, I want honesty. Can you handle that?" He questions me.

I can handle honesty, sure. I have no reason to lie. I already told myself I wanted to be his second chance. Looking deep into his eyes, I answer him. "I can handle anything you give."

Jake nods his head and smiles. "This is good. I'm beyond happy to hear this. And I'll do everything in my power to give you everything you deserve." He presses forward and kisses my forehead. Such a sweet gesture.



**It's been a** few days since Jake and I moved forward with our relationship. It's all new, but also exciting. I'm happy. Things seem to be going well for both of us. The connection between us seems to grow stronger every day. It's weird, really. When I'm with him, I feel perfect—but when he leaves or when I'm at work? It feels like a piece of me is missing. Sure, I've known Jake for years. Well, known of him really. But are there such things as soul mates? That's what Jake feels like to me. He's like a piece of my soul, you know that has been missing and I never realized it 'til now.

I have this sense in me that tells me to express my feelings that I have. Love. I know it is too soon, but I actually think I love him already. Crazy, right? Well, I guess I have never claimed to be normal.

I have two days off and think I'll do some cleaning today. Maybe go for a walk before Jake comes over.

I open the blinds in my living room to let the sun shine in and stand there. The warmth of it feels nice shining in on me. I sigh my simple content and bend down to open the window. A nice breeze would make it just perfect.

I head to the kitchen to pour myself a cup of coffee when my cell phone goes off.

I pick it up off the dining table and see a text from Jake.

**Thinking of you.**

I smile. Quickly, I respond to him.

**Oh really? In which way?** I smirk. I know I'm being a bad girl, but hey, there's just something with Jake that makes me want to be a little naughty with him.

**The naked way.**

Butterflies swim in my tummy. Excitement about his dirty thoughts thrill me. Never have I ever had a man think of me as beautiful, sexy or even worthwhile. I just hope I can keep his interest and earn his affections in a permanent way. Miracles can happen, right?

My fingers itch to attempt sexting, but I've never done that. I quickly rush to the kitchen and finish making coffee—which was my goal in the first place—and then go and sit on the couch with my phone in hand to respond.

**Naked? Where?** I bite my lip in anticipation of his answer.

**In front of me. Under me. Screaming my name in ecstasy.**

Shit. He's good. My pulse increases. Jake's good with words. He can turn me on with a simple text. I'm in so much trouble. Yikes.

I take a large sip of my coffee and set it down. With a deep breath, I try to come up with a response to that. I'm not great with words, but I'll try, that's for sure.

**What if I want you screaming my name?** I hold my breath. I don't know what his answer will be. I just threw that out there, digging. Curiosity. You know?

**Oh, blondie, if you only knew.** His text gives me the feels. It makes me wonder if his thoughts and feelings are mutual toward me. One can hope.

I need to end this chat before I need to go fix myself from sexual frustration. I need to distract myself from everything Jake for a little while and relax.

**Tell me later? Going to clean the bathroom** ☺

Yes, I smiley faced him, I don't want to be rude, but I don't want to leave him hanging either.

Sure thing, Devon. See you later.

I set my phone on the coffee table and finish my morning caffeine fix. After putting the cup in the kitchen I head to the bathroom to do some scrubbing.

I have the music blaring and a song I love comes on. I can't help but start dancing with the feather duster in my hand. Feeling good that all the cleaning's almost done I let loose. Twisting and twirling around my living room, I sing into the duster without a care in the world. I'm unaware of my surroundings until a crash of glass sounds and startles me. I scream. Looking in the direction of the sound, I notice that one of my front windows is smashed.

My guard comes up instantly and I look around assessing the situation. I run to the door and lock it. Looking out the window, I see no one—but a chill runs up my spine. I notice a rock laying on the floor under the window sill and move to pick it up. Looking it over, there's a note stuck to it. I pull it off and open it. We're watching you. My chest gets tight as my heart feels like it stopped and I can't breathe. The hairs on my neck stand up and my body starts to tremble. Quickly I set the rock on the table, and reach for my phone.

I dial quickly, and he answers on the first ring. "What's up, baby girl?"

"Mark, someone just threw a rock through my window." I tell my surrogate brother. Well, he did say we were family. I needed someone to call and he was the first person to come to mind. Shit. Jake. I should've called him.

"Stay put, Devon. I'm on my way." Mark tells me.

I end the call and begin pacing my living room. Who the hell would do such a thing? I haven't seen any kids wandering this area of the neighborhood. I don't remember pissing anyone off at the diner. I'm a bit freaked out. I better call Jake. I don't want to worry him.

I dial his number, but I get no answer. I guess I can just text him.

Jake, when you see this, come to my place asap, please. There's a problem and I need you.

I hope he doesn't get upset and I hope he's okay since he didn't answer his phone.

I sit on the couch, curling up and holding my knees close with my phone in hand.

I begin rocking back and forth on the couch and look through the window. I see a shadow by my front bush. It's not moving. Someone is there, just watching. My heart races as I stare, waiting to see if the said shadow will show itself. I swallow deeply and blink a couple times and the shadow's gone. Then a loud knock is at the door.

"Devon, it's Mark. Open up, baby girl." He shouts.

Quickly I jump up from the couch and rush to the door. Unlocking it and whipping it open. Mark walks in and shuts the door behind him. He takes me in his arms and my emotions get the best of me.

With my head pressed against his chest, the tears start to fall. Fear of the unknown does wonders to one's emotions.

"Shh, baby girl. I have you." He runs his hand up and down my back reassuring me. "Let's sit on the couch. Tell me what happened."

Mark lets me go and we both go sit on the couch. I resume my position of holding my knees, resting my chin on top of them as Mark sits right beside me.

"So?" He asks.

My body quakes, but I quickly calm myself. I need to get myself under control so I can explain what happened. "I was cleaning house. You know me. I need to have a tidy home." I chuckle with nervousness. "Anyways, the music was on and I was dusting. I guess I was distracted and then a loud crash happened." I looked at Mark and grimace. "I didn't see anything or anyone."

"Okay, and what broke the window?" He questions me, concern written all over his face.

I adjust my position and reach for the rock and note to hand to him. "This rock and note." I sit back again and watch for his reaction.

Mark turns the rock around in his hand a few times and then sets it on the table. He reads the note, his eyebrows narrow and his lips go tight. "Did you want to get the cops involved?"

I bit my lip then blow out a breath. Do I?

# CHAPTER FIFTEEN

*Jake*

I read the texts over again. I can't believe what I'm reading. Devon wants to hear me scream her name? I've corrupted the damn woman. Well, either that or my girl's not as innocent as she seems.

As I set my phone down I begin to imagine exactly what Devon wants. Vivid pictures come to mind and it's like an x-rated movie playing in my head. Damn, this woman is killing me. The things she makes me think, make me want to do to her.

I feel my cock getting hard, my pants getting tight. Fuck. I wish I was with Devon right now so I can sink myself balls deep into her. I grip my erection and groan. Later. Yes, I'll have her later, but for now, I really need a cold fucking shower.

Stripping from my clothes, I head towards the bathroom. I try and shake the pornographic thoughts from my head. Turning the knobs to cold, I get into the shower and let the freezing water do its job.

With my hormones tamed, I dress and head out to grab something to eat. I want to be fueled up and ready to roll when I get to Devon's. Our text banter has me wanting to give her my all. It sounds like she wants to play, and I'm game for that.

I stop in at the pizza joint just down the street. Grabbing a few slices, I sit and chow down. I guzzle a large mountain dew and now feel energized. The sky's the limit. I sure hope Devon is ready for me.

I don't want Devon to feel pressured with me showing up so early so I decide to head down to the pier. Sitting by the water used to be a thing I did to relax and get away from my father when things were really tough. Although it's been years, nothing has changed. I sit on a bench by the water and look out. The sun shines off the water, a small breeze blows, and birds chirp in the distance. The memories of my childhood have been suppressed over time, but just sitting here I can remember a few things.

I remember the first time my father beat Sean. When I tried to intervene, my father's hands came in my direction. Sean didn't get hurt as bad as I did—which I was glad for—but the fact that I couldn't protect him killed me. I always wished that Dom was around when this was happening, but he wasn't and it sucked. I tried every time to step in, and each time my father brought me back down to a lower level. Dirt. Connor Green's kids were dirt to him. He was the king and we were just lowly peasants, servants meant to serve his every need.

After a year of the increased beatings, I couldn't take much more. I did my best to keep Sean out of the way, but my father started sending me out on more tasks. By the time I got back, Sean was down for the count. The schools never did anything about the abuse. Sure, you could see all the bruises we both wore—there was no way we could hide them—but it seemed that everyone was afraid of my dear ol' dad. Either that, or he had some very special people that he paid off in times of need. I guess I'll never know.

When the stress of the life I was put into got to be too much, I began doing the odd drug to take the edge off. Blinders covered my eyes and before I knew it, Sean was part of the family business. I fucked up. I'd let our mother down. I let Sean down. I let myself down. Being so disgusted with myself over my fuck up, I let anger take over. And with that anger, came my life of crime. Some was okay, but when dad wanted people murdered, that was too far in my books.

A steamboat whistle startles me out of my memory flashback. I look at my phone to check the time. Two hours. Shit. I can't believe I have been sitting here, in a daze for two hours. I need to get to Devon.

I stand, dust off the back of my pants and head in Devon's direction.

It takes me half an hour to get to Devon's and when I get there, there's a police cruiser parked out front. My pulse kicks up a beat and I run to her front door. I rush in and see Devon sitting at her table talking with an officer and a few things in evidence bags. Some other guy sits on the couch drinking something. I look between the two in confusion.

"What happened?" I ask.

Devon looks over to me with a frown and then looks back to the officer and keeps talking as he writes.

The guy from the couch stands and comes over to me. He sticks his hand out. "You must be Jake. I'm Mark." We shake hands even though I still don't know who the guy is. I wait for him to explain.

"Yeah, I'm Jake. What's going on?" I ask a little more calmly.

"Someone threw a rock through Devon's window." Mark points toward the window and then the policeman. "After Devon called me, we decided to call the cops."

I look from the window to this Mark guy, and to Devon and back. I feel like I've been kicked in the stomach. Something happened to Devon and she called someone else? That doesn't seem right. Who's this damn guy?

"Mark? That's your name?" I ask. "Sorry, I don't know you. Who are you?" I put my hands in my pockets, feeling a little on edge, I don't want to do anything that I shouldn't.

Mark chuckles. "Oh, sorry. Yes, I'm like a brother to Devon. Been her boss and friend for years now. I own the diner." He smiles.

Instantly my guard drops. Brother. Boss. Friend. Okay, this I can deal with. But still, she didn't call me.

"Do we have any idea on who threw the rock?" I walk over to the couch and sit down. Not knowing how long Devon's going to be with the officer, I don't want to stand around looking like a jackass.

Mark comes and sits down as well. "No. But Devon mentioned that she saw a shadow out by the bush afterward." He picks up his mug and drinks. "Oh, there was also a note stuck to it."

What the fuck? A note? I feel my anger start to rise and need to push it down. I blow out a slow breath and lean forward putting my elbows on my knees, chin in my hands. There's nothing I can do at this point but wait. "Devon was mugged a couple weeks ago, and now this. Do you think they're related?" I turn my head and question Mark.

Mark shakes his head. "No, I don't think so. But I don't know enough to make that call."

I hear chairs scrap on the floor so I turn and see that Devon and the officer are just finishing up. Devon walks the officer out and then shuts the door.

I get up and go to her. I pull her into me. I hug her tight. "Are you alright?" I ask.

"Yes, I'm fine. Thanks." She says and pulls back. "I was shaken up, but doing better now."

I physically suggest she sit down beside Mark and I sit on the table in front of her. "If I'd known something was wrong, I would have come sooner, but you didn't call." I frown.

Devon bites her lip and looks down. She's either ashamed or hiding something from me, I don't know which.

"I did call you, you didn't answer. I even texted you. You didn't respond and I needed someone." She licks her lips—they look pretty dry. "Mark's like family so I called him and he came." She grimaces.

I pull my phone out and look at it. Shit. There is a little message thing on the top and missed call. How did I not see those when I checked the time? Fuck!

I reach my hands out and take hold of hers, reassuring her. "It's okay. I'm sorry. I must not have heard my phone or something. I wish I had. I need to start checking my phone after showers." I give her hands a little squeeze. "This relationship's new and I want you to know and get used to me being here, being there for you." I really want her to understand my meaning. I have failed one too many times in my life. I don't want to fail her.

Devon nods her head and gives me a small smile. "I will. I want that."

"Good."

Mark clears his throat as he stands. "Well, since the police are done, I'm going to head to the hardware store and get some plywood and nails. We need to board up the window until you can order a new one in Devon."

Devon stands and turns into Marks' arms. "Thank you so much, Mark. I'm glad to have you for family."

Mark leaves and it's just Devon and I. I'm still sitting on the table watching Devon pace the room. I have no idea what is on her mind right now, but I need to distract her, get her mind elsewhere.

"Blondie." I call to her. She stops and looks at me. "Come here, beautiful." I tell her. Reaching my hand out, offering myself.

Without any hesitation, she comes. I stand and take her into my arms. I hold her close, feeling her warm breath on my chest. I kiss the top of her head and press my chin there. Taking a breath, I pull back. Cupping both my hands to her face I look into her eyes. Smiling, I lean forward and press my lips to hers.

Her lips are warm and inviting. I want to devour her whole— but won't, not yet. I lick and nip her lips, her chin and down her neck. I try to be gentle and loving. Moving up, I start to nibble on her ear lobe and I hear her moan. Fuck me, Devon moaning is my undoing. I planned to go easy after the stress of her day, but now I don't think I can.

I lick, nip and tease some more—down her neck and around to her other ear. Back to her lips and she opens. Her tongue slips out and meets mine…and fuck me, it tastes like hot chocolate. It tastes so damn good. I dig in deep and lock on.

"Jake." Devon moans. "I want you."

"Oh, I want you too, baby. Boy, do I ever."

I'm worked up from the tongue teasing and don't think I can make it to the bedroom. I pull Devon close and pick her up, wrapping her legs around my waist. Moving us to the couch I lean down and lay her on the soft cushions.

"I can't wait, baby. I need you now. Here and now." I lean back and practically rip my shirt from my body. Needing to be free from the confinement of my clothing, I start to unbutton my jeans as Devon leans up and starts pulling her shirt off as well.

I stand and shove my jeans down to my ankles and kick them aside. I hear Devon panting, eager, just as I am. She's slower than I am with removing her clothes, so I help her. I take a hold of the waist of her pants and begin to pull them down her slim legs, feeling her shiver to my touch. She's not cold, that much I can tell. Her skin's hot to touch, and when I get her completely naked, things are just going to get hotter.

"Jake." She moans. I look up just as I toss her pants to the side. Devon tugs on her nipples, playing patiently, waiting for me. I smirk and dive right in. My mouth suckles on her toned stomach and I work my way up to her luscious breast. Taking one nipple into my mouth I suck and suck hard, letting it go with a pop.

I move to the other breast and repeat my actions. Devon moans the whole time. "Oh God, Jake." I peer up at her. She licks her lips and is breathing heavily.

I seat myself between her legs and begin to rub my hard cock against her now wet pussy. Fuck, I feel like I could blow my load already.

I tease her clit when I swipe back and forth. My hands roam freely, caressing her soft skin, up and down her torso, her hips, her breast. I can't get enough of her beautiful body.

The head of my cock slips in and shit. I have no condom with me. "Devon, baby. I'm clean." I kiss her freshly wet lips. "Are we good?" I kiss her again. I fucking hope we are good. After all this play, I don't think I can stop to run to her room to get a condom.

Devon's hands glide up my back and into my hair. She encourages me to look at her. "Yes, Jake. I'm clean too, so we're good." She pulls me down and devours my mouth with her warm lips and wet tongue.

I reach down and grab her leg—adjusting her body to fit me just perfect. Rubbing my cock against her pussy for lubrication, I slide right in. "Fu…uck! Devon, you feel so damn good." I groan as I push deeper inside.

Feeling like I hit a special spot, Devon begins to clamp down. Her pussy begins to tighten on each stroke I give—and man, it feels amazing!

Sweat pools between our bodies as we both wrestle for our climax. Devon's nails shear into my back every time I hit that wonderful little thing called the g-spot inside of her. I can feel her body shiver, and tense. Her breathing becomes erratic. She's constantly licking her lips, and I have no choice but to lick them for her.

Sucking her bottom lip into my mouth as I thrust hard and deep, I swallow her moans and my groan, my pleasure. This moment right here is true bliss. A feeling everyone should feel as I am sure they would never want it to end.

"Oh God, Jake. Jake. Jake. I… I…" Devon mumbles and then starts to scream. "Jake!" I feel her whole body tense, her pussy clamps down hard on my cock like it's trying to squeeze my load right out. I thrust once, twice and fuck.

"Fuck! DEVON!" I yell loudly.

I fall gently down over her and then curl to the side of her on the couch. With both of us satisfied, the couch feels like heaven. But then again, I'm a hot sticky mess right now, and could use a shower. I think a few minutes of downtime will be okay, though.

I reach my hand up and begin to brush Devon's hair out of her face. "Hey, blondie, you good?" I ask.

With a content smile on her face and a soft sigh, she looks to me. "I'm great."

I lean up on my elbow and look at my beautiful girl. "I never expected you. I mean, when I got out of prison, I planned on starting fresh, being a new man. I just never expected to find you." I kiss her forehead. "You are my sweet, blonde little angel. You're my redemption, Devon."

Her eyes glisten as she curls into me, hugging me. Her arms wrapped completely around my waist with head resting on my chest. She looks up to me. "I'm so very happy I can be that for you, Jake. I haven't been anything for anyone before." She swallows deeply and licks her lips. "I wasn't expecting you, either—but I am very happy you found me." She rests her head on my chest and becomes quiet.

Content. That is how I feel right now. Things are good. I'm starting over; I have a wonderful woman. I just hope things keep going in the right direction. I think I've atoned for my sins, not that I am a big believer in god and all, but I'm sure you know what I mean. I did my time, I learned my lesson. Time to move forward.

# CHAPTER SIXTEEN

*Devon*

I'm falling so hard for Jake. I never thought it'd be possible. After all this time in this crap city—going nowhere with my life— just by pure chance he walks into the place where I work and look where I am now. If you asked me a couple months ago if I thought I was ever going to be happy, I honestly don't know if I could have said yes. But now? I can say yes without a thought.

Jake makes me feel things I never thought were possible. He makes me feel beautiful. He lets me know that I'm thought about. He watches over me and proves that he cares. I haven't found any reason not to trust him—and of course, the sex is amazing.

We haven't discussed the fact that I'm friends still with his brother and sister in law. I'm not sure if I should mention that Jenn and I sometimes do lunch dates and that I've actually babysat his niece once or twice. That's a whole new can of worms.

I know Jake said he wants to make up for his regrets with Sean and Jenn. I wonder if I'll be able to help with that, like a mediator or something. We'll see.

I pull my head away from Jake's sweaty chest after a few minutes of silence. I hope he doesn't think I've fallen asleep. Oh, I'm sure I could've—but I didn't. I just was lost in thought.

I smile up at him. His gorgeous eyes glisten brightly at me. "Hey." I say.

"Hey back, blondie." He smiles.

I roll over and sit up on the side of the couch. "I think I'll go have a shower. Do you want to order some food and watch a movie?" I bite my lip with the question. I hope he says yes, I'm not ready for him to leave yet.

"Sure, baby. I could use a shower, too." Jake winks at me and gives me a wicked smirk. He starts to sit up and I don't know if he is looking to play more or what, but I giggle and jump up.

"Oh, is my poor baby a little dirty after playing?" I tease and smirk back.

Jake narrows his eyes at me and I know I'm in trouble. A slap on my ass from Jake and I start to run.

**I spent my** two days off with Jake and it was time well spent. Not a single minute was wasted. We had sex, we ate, showered, had more sex, watched movies and even went for a walk. We behaved like a young couple in love and I thoroughly enjoyed it.

Now it's time to go to work. The closing shift. I prefer to be with Jake—but then again, he doesn't pay my bills. I walk into the diner and it's rather busy. The bar's full up and there's only a single table empty. I'm surprised Mark didn't call me in early. I go and set my purse in the back and get right to work.

There must be a convention in the area because a lot of young couples keep coming in. By the time dinner hour comes, I'm exhausted. At least it has slowed down some and I can grab a quick bite to eat, too.

"Hey, Mark? Can you make me an order of fries, I'm starved." I call through the kitchen doors to my boss.

"Sure thing, baby girl." Mark says as he puts the finishing touches on the platter he is making. "You doing okay?"

I smile. "Yeah, I'm doing pretty good. Thanks." I walk back out to the dining room area and grab a cold drink. All the customers have been served and are eating so I have a few minutes to put my feet up. I sit on a stool and watch the crowd. If anyone needs anything I'm sure to see to them.

It's close to closing time, and my shift has sped by. The evening has gone by without a hitch. A lot of tourists came in and some regulars. Even these two guys that came in a little while ago that sort gave me the creeps came in, but they were good today. They might be becoming regulars. They like to flirt, that I know. I'll definitely have to keep my guard up with them.

Mark wanted to stay and close up, but I offered to stay so he and his wife could have some quiet time together. I've closed up many of times and had no problems, so why would tonight be any different? I say my goodbyes to him and my other co-worker and start my nighttime closing work.—shutting down the coffee machines, wiping the counters and such.

I have the kitchen finished, the lights off and am just finishing up the front area when I start to think about Jake. Daydreaming, you'd say. With my rag in hand, I stand at the counter in a daze.

I'm startled out of my thoughts by the bell of the door. I look up to see the men from early today. "Hey guys, how are you now? Did you forget something?" I ask them with a smile and stand up to walk around the counter. "Would you like a coffee or anything? It may be still warm." They both begin to approach me. One of the guys moves to the side of me as the other stops in front of me. I look at them. Something's wrong. The hairs on my neck stand on end. My pulse starts to race.

"No, bitch. We don't want no stupid coffee. We came here for you." The guy with the lip ring snarls.

Out of the corner of my eye I see the other guy coming up behind me. They have me trapped. The front and back doors are now blocked. My cell is in my purse. I have no idea what they want with me. "What do you want with me?" I ask softly trying to hide my fear. I look behind me and see that guy number two is only about a foot away. Looking back at guy number one I try and plead with my eyes. "Please don't hurt me. Just tell me what you want."

"Bitch, please. If you are friends with Jake, you are far from innocent. Stop being a cock-tease and get on your knees." He growls.

My breath catches. "Wh… what?" I mumble out.

"Get on your mother fucking knees bitch. NOW!" He yells.

I don't get a chance to move before the guy behind me knocks me to the ground. Slamming down hard on my knees, a jolt a pain rushes through me, I cry out in pain. Guy number one steps in front and grabs his crotch. "This won't suck itself, whore." He glares down at me.

Oh shit. No. No. No. This isn't good. This can't be happening. Think Devon. Fucking think. I take a deep breath. "Well, I'm not sucking it." I force out.

Dark spots cloud my eyes when his rough, meaty hand makes contact with my cheek. I fall to the floor. My jaw aches and I can taste a bit of blood in my mouth. I close my eyes and wait for the dizziness to go away. I can't let this happen. I have to fight.

"Are you ready to do as you are told, whore?"

I look up to the men, spit the blood out and wipe my mouth. "Go fuck yourself!" I shout to them. I can't be weak. I'll fight to my death if I have to.

One looks to two and laughs. "We have a feisty bitch on our hands, man. She thinks she's brave. Well, let's see what she can take." One says and nods to two.

I puff out heavy breaths of fear and anger when someone grabs my short hair and yanks me up to my knees. Once on my knees, they pull back my head and pull down my chin. I try to fight—but guy two leans on my legs, so my momentum is crap and my two arms are nothing compared to the four they have together.

I have my hands wrapped on guy twos arms, pulling on them, trying to get a release from my hair and face when something's shoved into my mouth. My eyes instantly look forward. I gag. I'm sure if it's from what's in my mouth or from knowing what's in my mouth. Guy one has put his dick in my mouth and is now looking at me with a smug look.

"Looks like you're sucking it, bitch. So suck!" He demands.

The hold on my chin and jaw is released slightly and the cock moves in and out of my mouth with forces. I gag as saliva fills my mouth. I want to vomit. Tears well up and start to fall down my cheeks. No, I can't let them win. No. I try to breathe in my nose and pull myself together. I hear the guy moan and mumble in co-errantly. The tension on my jaw vanishes and now's my chance.

It takes everything in me, but I reach up and grip his cock. "That's it. Suck it." He groans in pleasure.

I pull him back and lick the tip before sucking him back in. I moan and pretend I'm into it. I feel the tension on my hair loosen. I look up and see guy one's eyes close and it's time to strike. On the intake of sucking, I bite down hard on his cock, release and push him just enough to have space to turn and wrestle away from guy two who appears to rub himself through his pants.

"FUCK! Bitch! Grab her!"

I scramble away with what strength I have, but I don't get far. Guy two grabs me, smacks me across the face, pins me to the floor and waits for guy one.

"Let me go, you bastards!" I scream as I struggle. Kicking my legs and trying to free my arms from the prick above me.

"You are going to pay for that bitch." I hear as guy one stumbles over zipping up his pants with bloody hands. "If you think biting my cock hurts, wait until I'm finished with you." He growls as he lowers himself over my legs. He moves slowly up my body as guy two gets up, trading places.

I try to fight back as they switched, but they move too fast. It's a maneuver they have done once or twice before, you can tell. "Get off of me, asshole." I huff. With him now sitting on me with his weight, it's hard to breathe, therefore hard to talk.

"I think not. I think you owe me blood." The look in his eyes is something I have never seen. Not even on television. Such evil I don't think even existed until now. "Pike, give me your knife." He demands of guy two. At least I know a name of one. I need to keep that in my memory.

Tears fall from my eyes as I watch the guy named Pike hand no-name a big knife. He flicks it open and turns it on me. "Do you even know how to use that?" I ask, egging him on. I know I shouldn't, but I can't back down. I can't be weak. But damn it, I should shut the fuck up.

"Oh—those are fighting words, baby." He smirks as leans down and begins to slice open my shirt. "You have a sweet body under all these clothes. I see why Jake likes you." I can feel the knife on my skin as the blade slowly moves lower down my chest. "Perfect skin, perky tits, I would hate to mess it all up. But guess what, bitch? I told you, blood for blood."

The knife pierces the skin of my abdomen. I want to scream, but I fear that'd only make him enjoy it more. "Stop." I sob. The pain is so intense. It feels like he's cutting me from one end to the other. He probably is. I clench my eyes shut and pray he'd just end it already.

"Open your eyes, bitch!" I feel hot breath on my face. I open my eyes to see Pike's face hovering over mine. The lust I see in his eyes scare me. Blood turns him on and I'm in deep shit now. More than I thought possible.

I hear a whistle and look toward guy one. He holds the knife up with my blood dripping down. "That one's for my dick." He grins and his eyes sparkle. "What's funny is you didn't even realize you weren't pinned down anymore. What happened to the strong bitch?" He chuckles.

I quickly take stock and realize my arms are free, but before I know it, Pike pins them above my head and I let a few more tears leak out. "I'm strong asshole. I ain't dead yet, am I?" I sob. It takes everything in me to get that out. My breathing's erratic and my pulse is bounding. Panic and fear control me right now. I don't know if I'll get out of this alive or not, but I'll fight with my will and see what the outcome is.

The knife lands on my sternum and presses hard. "This one's for Jake taking someone from us." I wince. "Oh, and baby, you won't die today. We're just having some fun. We have a message for good ol' Jake for you to pass along."

The burn of the cut down my chest almost makes me pass out. I puff out breaths to try and stay alert. "What message?"

I feel a prick on my upper arm and I see stars. "…for thinking he can get away with it." The room begins to spin and my throat gets dry. I try to will my body to go numb. I don't want to feel it anymore. Each time he cuts, it feels like I'm being torn apart.

The room is getting dark. I have trouble keeping my eyes open. "Stay awake, bitch." One of them slams my head into the floor.

"Ahhh!" I scream and open my eyes. I try to focus on the men.

"You tell Jake that the boys are coming for him." He enunciates word for word as he slowly pushes the knife into my left shoulder.

I scream as the most pain possible hits me with each word and each inch the knife goes. I scream so much I can't hear myself anymore—I'm deaf from it all. Everything is blurring in front of me. Beside me—tables, chairs. I see a large, bloody fist just as things begin to fade completely.

# JEAN KELSO

# CHAPTER SEVENTEEN

*Jake*

Back at the hotel as I lay on the bed, I can't shake the feeling that something bad is going to happen. The fact that, that guy Snake was in the diner the other day, so soon after running into me seems too suspicious to me. The other guy with him did seem somewhat familiar, but I'm not sure from where. And now a window has been smashed at Devon's. I don't know if two and two go together in this situation, but it sure doesn't feel right. It has been a long time since I have dealt with anyone from my past, and I never did deal one on one with my father's outer connections. A chill runs up my spine. I grunt to myself. Fuck this.

Rolling off the bed I strip myself of my clothing and head to the bathroom. Maybe a nice hot shower will help. I can't seem to stop my thoughts from running amiss.

I'm so tense. The hot water does nothing for me. After getting dressed I try to text Dominic, hoping that he still has the same number he did seven years ago. I need to know who this 'Snake' guy is. My gut is sinking fast, and if anyone can tell me about the fucker it'd be my oldest brother. Dom's a dark fucker who's the one who should've spent some jail time, but seems to be everywhere but where someone needed him. But he's my brother and I do love him. He was dealt a shit life too, he just adapted better than the rest of us.

Five minutes. Ten. Fifteen minutes, and I'm wound so tight I can't take it any longer. I look at the clock, it's almost closing time, so I shove my feet into my shoes and head out the door. I need to check on Devon. I can't let anything happen to my woman. Did I

95

just say, my woman? Fucking right, I did. She's my one chance. My redemption at life and I will not let her down.

With my mind set, I head right to the diner. The closer I get, the worse I feel. It's a few minutes past closing time and when I finally approach the door the open sign is still on. My heart begins to race. I take a deep breath and open the door. The place has an eerie silence. A few steps in I call out. "Devon?" I get nothing in return. I get past the first booth and I catch something out of my peripheral vision so I look and there she is.

"No…" I scream and run towards her lifeless looking body. There's blood. More than I like to see. I fall to my knees. "Devon? Devon baby, wake up." I start to assess her body for injuries. I notice the knife right off. I don't pull it—I don't know what internal injuries she might have. Swallowing deeply, I close her shredded shirt as I look at the cuts across her chest and torso. Tears begin to well up in my eyes. I check for a pulse and she has one. It's slow and weak, but it's there. I reach into my back pocket and pull out my phone. Quickly I dial nine-one-one. "Hold on, baby. Help is coming."

**Sitting in the** waiting room, rage and fear both consume me. This is my fault. I should've trusted my gut feeling. I knew something was wrong. I should've gone to her earlier. The fact that those guys were at the diner wasn't a coincidence at all. How could I have been so stupid? Fuck! Now my sweet angel lays on a stretcher with God knows what kind of injuries and it's because of me—because of my fucked up past. Will I ever be able to outrun it? I don't want to be that man anymore. How many times do I have to say it?

Time moves too slowly. The doctors haven't come back out to give me an update. I need to know that Devon's okay. I look around the room and see several other people waiting, probably feeling just as stressed as I am. How hard is it to give a simple update? Fuck! I'm going to lose my mind if a doctor doesn't come out soon.

I stand up and begin to pace the room. Tension begins to build in my muscles. I clench my fists and unclench. I need to relieve the tension. I need answers.

"Mr. Green?" I hear and stop in my tracks. Looking around, I find the voice.

"That's me." I say and walk toward the woman in a lab coat. "Is she okay? Please tell me she's okay." I stare at the woman, praying with everything that's mighty that Devon is going to fine.

"She's stable right now. We need to take her up to surgery to remove the knife, the lacerations on her body weren't too deep, so we were able to clean them up and stitch them." The doctor tells me. And it feels like a weight is slowly being lifted off my chest.

"So, she'll be okay then?" I ask, looking at the doctor's name tag. "After the surgery, Devon will fine then, Dr. Godwin?"

Dr. Godwin puts her hand on my shoulder and smiles. "Yes, she'll be just fine. If you want to go up to the fifth floor and wait in the ICU waiting room, Devon will be admitted there after surgery." She pats my shoulder twice and walks off.

Relief overcomes me, so much so that I have to sit down. The stress of everything that has happened…the fact that I wasn't there for my sweet angel to protect her causes extreme guilt. But knowing she'll be okay makes me feel better. Sitting in the closest chair, I lean over and put my head in my hands. I blow out long deep breaths. I'm beyond happy at this moment. I never thought I could feel such relief. Devon's going to be okay. Now I just need to make up for this horrible situation. But how?

I take a few minutes to collect myself and then I head to the elevators. Riding up to the fifth floor I think to myself on what I want to say to Devon. What could I possibly say really? Did I really think my past would come to hurt me or anyone else? I hope it didn't. Can I fix my past? No, I can't. Can I honestly protect her? I will do everything in my fucking power to do so.

The elevator dings, alerting me that I've hit my destination. I exit and look for signs to show me where I need to go. Once I find the waiting room to the intensive care, I make myself as comfortable as I can in the uncomfortable looking chairs and wait. I don't know how long Devon's surgery's going to be, but I'll sit here for as long as it takes. I need to see her. I need to see with my own two eyes that my woman's okay. When I saw her last, she looked like death warmed over. Seeing that knife sticking out of her killed me inside. Her skin was pale with spots of blood all over, with her shirt torn open and her breasts exposed.

I squeeze my eyes closed needing to shake the vivid picture that just popped inside. I don't ever want to see Devon that vulnerable again. I plan to find Snake and I'll kill that mother fucker if it's the last thing I do.

What? No. Wait. I can't do that. Fuck! But I really want to. I shake my head. So many conflicting thoughts. I pull my phone out and start to scroll the internet for cat videos, anything silly or weird. I need something to distract me. I need something happy, and I remember Devon telling me once that cat videos always made her smile.

# CHAPTER EIGHTEEN

*Devon*

I'm tired, groggy and my eyelids feel like they have weights sitting on them. I swallow and it feels like sandpaper. My mouth's so dry. I try to lick my lips but there's no moisture to dampen them. I manage to get my eyes open and everything is a blur. My whole body aches, but my chest and left shoulder hurt the most. It feels like there's something heavy sitting beside me so I lift my right arm and try and brush off what's causing the extra weight on my left side. But something stops me before I can.

A warm hand touches my wrist and a familiar voice speaks. "It's okay, Devon. That's just a dressing." He says. I look over to the person and wait for my vision to clear. Jake.

"Jake? They... they..." I try to tell him that the men had a message—but my voice is garbled, and my throat's sore.

Jake brushes the hair off my forehead and with his other hand takes a hold of my right hand. "Shh, baby. It's okay. Don't try and talk yet. You just got out of surgery. Rest a bit and we can talk after." His voice is soft and he sounds so concerned for me. His feelings show full blast with his compassion and empathy. I let a tear escape and run down my face. Jake wipes it off instantly and kisses my forehead. "Rest, baby. I'll be right here when you wake up."

I close my eyes as Jake requests, but sleep doesn't come. Flashbacks play over and over in my mind. I can't believe I'm alive after it all. The brute force those men used—like it was all a game to them. The pain they caused me. Such animals in a messed up world.

I hear Jake whisper to someone, but I'm not sure who to. He must be on the phone. Footsteps come toward me and chair scrapes along the floor.

"You awake, baby?" Jake whispers to me.

I moan in my groggy state and open my eyes. Turning my head to him I nod. "Yes."

Jake takes my hand closest to him and gives it a squeeze. "I just talked to Mark. I caught him before he left for work. He says that the diner will be closed for the day. And he's coming up. He said he needs to check on you. Needs to see you with his own eyes." Jake shakes his head and chuckles. "Damn, man can't take my word that you are okay."

I smile at him and return his hand squeeze with what strength I have. Although I have been working with Mark for years, I'm just now learning how much I mean to the man. When he said we're family, I guess he really meant it.

"Well, that's what big brothers do, right? Plus, the police will make the diner a crime scene, won't they?" I try and shift in the bed to get a little more comfortable. The numbness from obvious pain medicine starts to wear off. "Can I have a drink, please?"

Jake's up and out the door in a flash—only to return with a glass of something a few minutes later. He sits back down beside me and grimaces. "The nurses say you can only have ice for now, so they gave me a cup of ice chips. And yeah, they will. They will probably do a once over of the place and Mark will be back in business." He holds the cup in front of me in a form of an offering.

I try to maneuver myself to reach the cup, but the pain is getting bad. Jake must notice that something's wrong as he takes a piece of ice and brings it up to my dry lips.

"Open up, blondie. Let's see how you do with this." He slips the ice in my now open mouth and I feel instant relief.

The cold feeling is refreshing and with the ice melting, it tastes delicious. My mouth and throat are so dry. I never realized that taking ice for granted before was a thing. Like water for example. I understand completely now when they use the expression of being drier than the Sahara Desert. I move the ice about in my mouth and savor it down to the last drop.

"Can I have another please?" I ask Jake. He immediately slips another piece in my mouth and I begin to suck on it.

"I know now's not a great time, Devon—but the police will be around soon." Jake narrows his eyes and frowns. "Do you know who did this to you?" He asks.

Hell, yeah I do. I instantly swallow the little chip of ice and nod. "Yes! I don't know their names, but they were customers from the diner."

I can see Jake tense up beside me, his eyes darken. "What do you mean? Customers? Like some of your regulars?" His voice sounds upset.

I shake my head slowly. Worried that Jake will freak out thinking that some of my sweet regulars could possibly do such a thing. "Heck, no. These guys just started coming in the past two weeks." I bite my lip trying to remember details of their looks. "One guy I remember has long hair, kind of greasy looking, skinny with some tattoos. And the other guy's a bit stockier and had a ring in his lip. I overheard one of them say the name Pike, but I can't be sure. They both give me the willies when they come in the diner, but customers are customers."

Jake's eyes close shut and I can hear his teeth grind. "Fuck!" He grunts through his clenched teeth.

This isn't good. Jake is angry for sure. He must know who the guys are. Well, obviously they knew him since they wanted me to give him a message.

"Umm, Jake." I whisper.

He blows out a breath and looks down at me. "Yeah, baby, what do you need?"

I swallow deeply, unsure if I should tell him or not. But I know if I don't tell, things could turn out bad. "They wanted me to tell you…" I take a breath. "To tell you that the boys are coming for you." I bite my cheek and wait. I hope I'm right in telling him.

Jake stands before he leans down and kisses my forehead. "Thank you for telling me. I'll take care of this, Devon. Get better soon, baby." And he walks out the door. He doesn't look back. Nothing. He's just gone.

Did I just screw up?

# CHAPTER NINETEEN

*Jake*

Seeing my woman looking all bruised up, with cuts on her precious skin, now covered with bandages and a sling on her arm, slices me deep. And to find out that it's my past that caused all that? Well, fuck me. That stings like no other sting. When she described the men with that little bit of detail, I knew. Dom's lackeys. I need to find that fucker of a brother of mine and have him help deal with his freelancing men. If not, I might be back behind bars before the night is over.

I can't tell Devon my thoughts on this, so I just lean down and kiss her head before I leave. If I sit there any longer, my anger will build and shit will hit the fan so fast, the fan will land on Devon again and it'll be my fault again. I can't let that happen. I need to take care of this, and I need to do it now.

As soon as I'm out the hospital doors, I pull out my cell phone. I call for a cab and begin to think of some of the old haunts Dom used to hide.

The cab pulls up and I jump in. I give him the address to the first place and we are on our way.

Six hours later, I've lost count of how many stops the cabbie and I have made. Not a single place shows any reminder of Dom and the men that are around the area don't even look familiar. Sure I ask if they know him or had seen him, but nothing. It's like my big brother has disappeared off the face of the earth…but that isn't possible unless he is dead. That's a possibility, too—but that would suck.

I have the cab driver bring me to my hotel and pay him the large amount owed. I'm starving at this point, but more exhausted than anything. My defeat now drowns out my anger. I strip out of my dirty clothing and head to the bathroom.

I look in the mirror, my eyes dark and skin pale. This day sure has taken a toll on me. I can't imagine how Devon's feeling. Fuck. Devon. My poor, sweet girl. I close my eyes and picture her battered body and a surge of anger hits. Clenching my fist, I pull back and slam it into the mirror, smashing it to pieces. Blood starts to trickle down my fist and arm, but I don't feel any pain. I'm numb.

Leaving the broken mirror as is, I turn and start the shower. With my head down, I stand under tepid water waiting for it to heat up. My hands press on the wall and blood flows down the drain. I leave the shower curtain open so I can see what my rage does to me, a reminder for myself to stay calm, relax.

The water heats up to almost scalding and I let it rain over my aching body. Being tense all day from anger does a number on your muscles. I bring my cut up hand under the water and begin to pick out pieces of broken mirror, tossing out of the shower into the sink across the way.

All the glass is gone. There are just a few cuts on my knuckles. It doesn't look too bad, but I know my hand will bruise up. Just another reminder. I blow out a breath and grab the soap and begin to wash off the remints of the late night and early day.

Feeling as clean and calm as I'll ever be, I turn the water off and grab the towel. I wrap it around my waist I step out, being sure not to step on any glass that may have landed on the floor. I head out to the living area and sit on the bed. I feel stupid for letting my anger taking control. That's something the old me used to do. I'm finally heading somewhere new—better—in this life and I have to go and fuck it up. I should've just stayed at the hospital with Devon and let the police deal with it. But no. Once a fuck up, always a fuck up. Right?

I dry off and dress in some pajama pants. I want to go back to the hospital, but I'm worn out. I should have a clear head before seeing Devon, so I pull the blankets back on the bed and crawl in.

**I wake to** the sun shining through the window. It's bright and it makes me smile. I slept all evening and through the night. I must've needed it. I feel much better today, my anger is gone and I just want to see Devon. I hope the police weren't too hard on her and maybe they'll have an update on the case this morning.

I pull my pajama pants down and off, tossing them aside and pull out a pair of faded blue jeans from the drawer. I pull them up and open the next drawer. Digging through the shirts, I find a nice tight gray tee and slip it on. Hey, don't hate. I need to suck up a little to my woman for walking out like I did, so looking good can't hurt.

Slipping on my shoes, I grab my wallet and head out. I stop at the closest coffee shop and grab a cup to go and call for a cab. The hospital is across town and I don't want to waste the time walking.

Standing on the sidewalk, sipping my coffee, my mind begins to wander. Visions of Devon battered and bruised appear and I try to shake them. I force my mind to picture her beautiful smile, her pixie like hair, her bright eyes, soft skin, clear of any marks and it works. Relief flows through me and I'm startled by a honk. The cab is parked in front of me and I didn't even realize it.

I open the door and get in. "Sorry, man. I sort of spaced out there." I chuckle.

"Not a problem." The man responds. "Where to?" He asks.

I think quick, trying to remember the name of the hospital remembering there is more than one in the city. "Uh, Saint John's Providence I believe. Thanks." I smile to the eyes peering at me in the rearview mirror.

"Sounds good. Be there shortly." He says and pulls away from the curb.

Traffic is light this morning, which makes the drive pretty quick. We pull up in front of the hospital in under twenty minutes. I pull my wallet out, pay the nice man and get out. "Thanks, man."

Walking into the hospital I look up at the signs to reorient myself to where the ICU was and head in the direct they say.

I get to the waiting room of the intensive care and see the doors shut. There's a phone by the doors so I pick it up. It rings and someone answers. "Intensive care, can I help you?"

Feeling stupid (since I walked right in yesterday) this is new to me. I go with the flow. "I'm here to see Devon."

"Does Devon have a last name?" The voice asks.

I draw a blank. Shit. Last name. I rack my brain for a name. I honestly can't remember one. I don't think she gave me one, and me being a stupid shit, didn't ask. Fuck me. "I'm sorry I don't know. She is a patient of Dr. Godwin. I was here yesterday. My name is Jake." I pray the little bit of information is enough to gain access. I really want to see my girl.

"One moment please." The voice states firmly. It sounds annoyed actually which I understand. How stupid can one person be? I'm the damn boyfriend and don't know my own girlfriend's last name. I smack my forehead in disbelief.

I start to pace the hall, all hope beginning to dwindle as the minutes go by.

The doors open and Mark walks out. This can't be good.

I rush toward him. "Hey, man, how is she?" I ask, my words rushed and worried.

Mark takes hold of my shoulders and stops me dead. "You fucking walked out on her?" Anger present and heavier with each word. "How could you do that? Jesus fuck, Jake! What the hell?" Mark shakes me a little and steps back. He shakes his head and blows out an angered breath.

I put my hand on my neck and begin to rub. Stress begins to build up again already. "Mark, man. I needed to get out. My anger was boiling over. I know who did it." I look up to the heavens and breath heavily. I need to keep my cool. I look back at Mark. "Is she pissed?" I grimace.

"Fuck, yeah. She's upset man. She needed you last night. She was up all night with nightmares. And then there was the pain. Jesus, man." Mark clenches and unclenches his hands, then shakes them out. "Then the nurse approaches me and says a guy named Jake is asking about Devon, but doesn't know her last name. Who the fuck are you man? Men should know their women's last names." Mark reaches out quick and smacks me across the head. I didn't realize what he was doing until it was too late.

"Owe." I rub my head for a second. "What the fuck man."

"Prix."

I look to Mark confused. "What?"

"Prix."

"Prix what, man?" I ask. Why does he keep saying the same thing over and over?

Mark sighs loudly. "Her last name, you twit. Prix. Devon Prix. Don't fucking forget it."

Well, damn. Do I feel stupid now? "Prix. Gotcha!"

Mark starts toward the door. "Now, that we got that over with, you coming in to see her, or what?"

Finally, I get to see my girl. "Damn straight." I head toward the door as Mark calls in and the door opens.

# JEAN KELSO

# CHAPTER TWENTY

*Devon*

A nurse came in the room fifteen minutes ago and pulls Mark out. I don't know where he went or why, but it's awfully quiet in here now. I don't like the quiet. It makes me think about everything again. It gives me time to wonder where Jake went. Why he left and to wonder if he is okay.

The nurses have been rather routine with the pain medicine, but the doses have been minimal. I still feel so much, so sleep hasn't been good. Because of the pain, the nightmares haven't been nice. I can't get my attackers faces out of my mind. When the police officers came in yesterday I was in so much pain, it was hard to remember all the details, so they said they'd return in a day or two when things were a little better to get more information. The one officer said they might bring a sketch artist with them.

Mark arrived not long after Jake left me yesterday bringing my purse from the diner and hasn't moved from my side. Poor Emily has been taking over many of the diner duties on her own, and I feel bad for that. I told Mark to go home last night, but he said that since Jake wasn't here, that he wasn't going anywhere. I of course cried. Mark. The family I never knew I had all this time.

I use my good arm to grab the cup of water that I now can have, and sip a mouth full through the straw. I hear the door open and look over as I set the cup down. In walks Mark, and behind him, is Jake looking nervous as hell.

A weight lifts from my chest seeing him there. He looks good. Tired, but good. Sexy actually, makes me wonder if he's trying to butter me up for something.

Mark goes and grabs his jacket that he brought. He walks over to me and takes my hand. "I'm going home to my beautiful wife and going to make sure the diner is still standing now that the police are done their business there." He grins, and leans down and kisses the top of my head. "I'll check on you later, baby girl."

I smile as I watch him walk out. The door closes and I look to Jake. He stands by the door still, looking unsure whether it's okay to be here or not. I'm upset with him, but I was more worried than anything.

"Come sit with me, Jake." I nod to the chair beside the bed.

Jake walks over and sits down. He takes my hand and begins to rub his thumb over my skin. "How are you?" He asks, his voice low, but full of concern.

I shift in the bed trying not to wince when the pain strikes. "I'm a little better today, thank you. How are you?" I ask. I really do want to know if he is doing alright. I want to know that I didn't screw up by telling him what the guys wanted me to tell him.

He looks me dead in the eye. His eyes dull and blank, with wrinkles at the corners. His lips are stiff and his nose is flaring, I see his regret. "I'm sorry for leaving yesterday. I let my anger get the best of me and I hurt you in the process." He frowns and blows out a long breath. "Hurting you is the last thing I want to do, Devon."

I can see the pain and regret sitting in front of me. His words of apology—I know he's telling me the truth. I know he has a past, a past he is trying to atone for. Jake wants to move forward, not backward.

I honestly don't know how to physically comfort him while lying in this bed right now. I wish I was home, uninjured so I could show him that everything will be okay, but I just don't know. What I do know is that I want him, and I'll do what I can to make it work.

"I know, Jake. We'll take it one day at a time. Work at things together. Manage each obstacle as they come." I smile at him.

A small smile appears on Jake's face. "So…am I forgiven?" He asks.

That little smile makes him look so innocent, only I know he's anything but. I bite my lip and smirk. "Hmm, let me think about it."

His smile disappears and he sits up straight in the chair, removing his hand from mine. He looks like he's in shock, not realizing I'm teasing.

I reach for his hand again and squeeze. "I'm teasing, Jake—geez. Yes, you're forgiven, silly."

He blows out a breath. "Fuck, Devon. I really thought you were upset."

He seems genuinely upset over it, now I feel bad. "I'm sorry, Jake. I guess now isn't really the time to play around, eh?" I look down to our joined hands and think about nothing in particular.

When I look up, he has a sincere expression present, and his eyes bright. "You can play around any time, blondie. It's me, not you. I'm just messed up. My emotions are a wreck over the fact that my past has come between us and has gotten you hurt. It's something I never wanted to happen." He leans toward me and his lips touch mine softly.

His lips are warm, soft and I want more than just a little touch. I press my lips onto his harder telling him what I want. I hope he wants the same. It feels like a lifetime since we have been close and his touch would make me feel better right now.

Jake pulls back. "Whoa, baby, slow down. We're in the hospital and you are still injured. I'm not saying no—I'm saying wait 'til you are better." He looks me up and down, my battered body, laying in the damn bed with rails and sanitized sheets. Ugh. I bet I'm a sight for sore eyes. I probably wouldn't want to kiss me either.

I sigh. "No, I get it, Jake. It's okay." I move my good arm to my lap and start of pick at the nails on my bad hand, an old nervous habit of mine. "I hope I get to go home soon." I look to him feeling sad and lonely. Even though he's sitting right here with me, I still feel alone. He gets to leave and I have to stay.

"I can talk to the doctors for you and see if we can get you out of here sooner than later." He raises his eyebrows in question. He looks to the door and back. "I can go ask right now. I'd do that for you, anything to make you happy, Devon." He starts to stand.

I reach out to stop him. I love the fact that he's willing to do that, but the police officer is coming tomorrow and I don't want him to have to chase me down to get my statement. "No, Jake, that's okay. They might let me leave after giving my statement tomorrow. Let's just wait one more day, okay?" I smile, hopefully with enough reassurance to keep him seated.

I just get him to stay when a knock on the door makes us both look.

The door opens slowly and in walks Sean. My heart stops, and my chest tightens. The biggest secret I have been holding from Jake is now being revealed. Shit. I look to Jake and he is still staring at the doorway.

The door closes and no one speaks. I think we are all in utter shock. I look from Jake to Sean and I think the stress of the situation hits me too hard, tears start to drip down my face. The stress and fear are overwhelming. What is going to happen now? Are they both going to hate me?

"Jake? Sean?" I call out, not sure if either can hear me in the utter silence of the room. I assess their reactions again and call out once more. "Jake? Sean?"

Both men finally look to me, their expressions confused—but also angered.

I'm lost for words. Do I apologize or just start explaining everything? Fuck, I should have told both of them about each other from the beginning.

"Sean, how are you?" I utter out the first words.

Sean looks from me to Jake and back. "Why the fuck is my brother here, Devon? Actually, how the hell do you know him in the first place? Jesus Christ, woman!" He yells.

"Hey, don't be yelling at her like that." Jake butts in.

Sean looks to Jake and snarls. "You shut your mouth. You don't need to talk right now. I'm talking to Devon. Wait, no. Actually, Jake, what the fuck are you doing out of jail? I was never notified of your release." Sean's hands are moving a mile a minute with all his questions. Shit, he's angry. I try and tuck myself back further in the bed and let the shit storm begin.

Jake stands up. "I'm out on parole, Sean. Not my fault you weren't notified. And Devon's my woman. Shit!" Jake shouts and runs his hands through his hair. "Look, Sean. I don't want to fight man. I'm not that man anymore. Just give me a chance." Jake's hands move to his pockets and he settles back down in the chair.

"Woman? Your woman?" Sean mumbles and looks to me. "Is he serious, Devon? Are you two a couple?"

I swallow the large lump I feel in my throat, try to sit up taller with much difficulty and pain and look directly at Sean. I can't be little shy Devon anymore. I'm a grown woman. I have a backbone and I need to use it, like I did with those men. "Yes, Sean, we are. Jake isn't who he used to be. He's changed."

Sean goes and sits on the unused chair in the room. He rests his head in his hands and leans on his knees. I can tell he's frustrated. Sean and I have talked over the years about his feelings for his brother. He told me that if he ever had the chance, he'd try and mend fences if it was possible…but it'd take a lot of mending. But was that all talk? Now that they are face to face can that actually happen?

113

# JEAN KELSO

# CHAPTER TWENTY-ONE

*Jake*

Sean's here. I can't fucking believe my own brother—my biggest regret—is in this very room right now. What I want to know is how Devon and Sean are friends still? Devon said they were friends in school, but she never said they were friends still. Fuck. What a way to come face to face with another part of my past. I wanted this part to be dealt with on my own, not with Devon in the middle. But I guess I can't have everything, can I?

I'm angry that Devon kept her friendship with him a secret, but our relationship is still fresh. I have to give her time to tell me these things…but it also makes me wonder if there are other secrets she may be holding back.

I watch Sean sit in the chair across the room. His frustration's being made known to both of us. I know he's angry, too.

I don't know what to say. I told him already I'm not the same. Devon told him I've changed. I look over at Devon and she is already looking at me. She is frowning, worried. She wears her emotions on her sleeve, that's for sure.

"Hey, Jake, do you mind taking off for a bit? Give Sean and I some time?" She raises her eyebrows and gives me puppy dog eyes.

Well, damn those eyes. She hasn't used those before and they're hard to resist. Damn it! "Yeah, blondie. I'll come back in an hour or so." I get up from the chair, lean over the bed and kiss her forehead. I look to Sean one more time and leave the room. I sure hope Devon can talk Sean off the ledge. Maybe in the near future my brother and I can sit and have a normal discussion.

I'm just about to the doors of the hospital when I hear my name. Well, at least I'm sure it was my name, the noise level at the entrance is loud. I look around but see no one familiar until I see her. Shock, utter, complete shock overcomes me. Jenn.

She hasn't changed much since I last saw her. Regret and pain rack me as I watch her walk toward me.

With just a few feet separating us, she looks me up and down, a small frown present. She pushes her purse up on her shoulder. "When did you get out of jail?" She asks me quite bluntly.

Taken back with the force of her question, I put my hands in my pockets so I don't reach out and touch her. "Almost a month or so now. How are you, Jenn?" I ask as I rock back and forth on the balls of my feet.

Jenn shakes her head and grimaces. "I'm good. I shouldn't be talking to you, Jake—but it's been a long time, and Sean has told me several stories of the life you both grew up with." She licks her lips and blinks a couple times. "I've had time to come to terms with things and I swore to myself if I ever saw you again, I'd forgive you."

Forgive me? I'm stunned. This sweet, beautiful woman's willing to forgive me for my past mistakes when I haven't even forgiven myself. Sean sure struck gold with this woman. The feel of my heart jumping in my throat strikes—fear that this is only a dream flashes quickly. "How can you forgive me for all the crap that I've done, Jenn. I was horrible to you, to Sean?" I swallow the large lump like feeling in the throat. Just those simple words have my emotions on overdrive.

I glance around, checking my surroundings. I need verification that this isn't a dream. Looking back at Jenn, I see she has stepped closer.

"I don't even forgive myself, Jenn. I have so many regrets— so many things to make up for, if I can." I tell her, stumbling over my words.

116

Jenn steps even closer, her arms raising until her hands settle on my shoulders. Her touch sends a chill through me. "You may not forgive yourself yet, Jake—but you will. Just give yourself time. From what Sean has told me, you were once a good man, and you can be that man again. But…" She pauses.

Her skin is warm and soft. I know this is for real. I can feel her. I can smell her slight vanilla scent now that she's closer, and her eyes shine with honesty. No hate, no fear shows in her appearance. "But what?

She smiles. "But you have to want it…to want to be that man, to fight for it, Jake. Are you strong enough to handle that?" Her questions fall from her lips as if she knows what's going on in my mind. She's asking all the right things and I have the answers because I do want it. I want it so bad, and I hope it's possible.

"I want it. I can do it. I *will* do it." I squeeze her hands and smile. "You have gotten awfully smart over the years, Jennifer Samos." I smirk.

"Green. It's Jennifer Green now. Sean and I are married, Jake. And we have a daughter, Sofie. She's six, almost seven."

Well, shit—hearing it from her makes it realer. I'd heard rumors through the mill. Knowing that they were living a happy life always helped me get through my time, but hearing it first hand? Man, I have missed so much. Fuck, I'm an asshole.

I pull her in for a hug, praying that it's okay to do so. Once she's wrapped in my arms, she returns the hug. No flinches and no shutters. Just plain warmth. Damn, I'm a wuss. Pulling back, I sniff. Feeling so emotional, I hold back the tears that build up. "I'm so happy things worked out for you both, even with everything I did. Everything our family did."

Jenn sets her hands on her hips and sasses me. "Did you really think I'd let Sean get away that easily?" She smiles big and then giggles. "I let him go once. I wasn't letting that man go again. But thank you, Jake. We're not letting anything get in our way of happiness."

I nod my head, my hands back in my pockets. My chest feels less heavy, but I know things won't be as easy with Sean. "I'm so glad we had this chat, Jenn. I hope someday Sean will feel the same way."

"He'll get there. Leave him to me." She looks to her wrist, a watch, must be checking the time. "Anyways, I must go find Sean. I just dropped Sofie off at school, and we have some running around to do. It's good to catch up, Jake." She leans in and gives me a soft kiss on my cheek. "See you again." And she walks off.

Still in shock, I walk out of the hospital with nowhere in mind to go. I think I'll just wander the streets and clear my mind. So much has happened already. I've found a woman I'm falling for, and have been forgiven for a piece of my past. I feel like I'm dreaming. I must be. Yes, I'm still in prison, laying in my cot, in my cell, dreaming about a possible future.

# CHAPTER TWENTY-TWO

*Devon*

"Sit down, Sean." I tell him. The only way to get this stubborn man to listen is to make him. I've known Sean for many of years and this wasn't the way I wanted him and Jake to reunite. But damn if the timing of visits were as they were. Stupid karma. Lady karma wanted this to happen, I know it. And now I have to try my damndest to fix it.

Sean paces the room with a sneer on his face. "I don't want to sit." He growls.

Stupid men. "Sit the fuck down." I return his growl. My own anger rises with his stubbornness. If he wants to be a jerk, I'll be one too. "You'll listen to me and you will listen well. Now sit!"

With a loud puff of air, he stomps to the chair and sits. He looks to me with a raised eyebrow. "Now what?" Sarcasm noted.

"Oh, don't be a jackass." I shift in the bed, angling myself to face him better. "Look, I know you weren't expecting to see Jake here."

Sean cuts me off with a fierce look and another growl. "Expecting? Seriously, Devon? My fucking brother who's supposed to be in prison…"

I cut him off by correcting him. "He's on parole."

"Okay, fine—who's on fucking parole for all the crap he did in the past—is in your hospital room saying he's your what? Your boyfriend? And you want me to be happy? Fuck that!" He shakes his head. Frustration fills the room.

Sighing I reach for my glass of water and take a sip. I already want to bash my head against a wall. Sean's skull's so thick, I

119

don't know what'll get through to him, but I damn well will try my hardest.

"He knows he fucked up, Sean. He wants to make up for his mistakes. He isn't the same person he was years ago. Plus, you weren't always innocent, remember?" I take another sip and set my glass down.

Sean stands and looks at me. I glare at him and he succumbs to my force and sits back down. "He looks the same to me." The pouty lip I've heard about from Jenn appears. Jenn told me he uses it to try and get his way. Well, it won't work on me.

"Looks don't mean shit, and you know it. Why won't you give him the chance to work things out with you? Seven years is a long time to think about your mistakes."

Sean's cell phone goes off and he pulls it out of his pocket. He looks at it and then to me. "Jenn's here, she'll be up in a few minutes."

"Oh, where's Sofie?" I ask.

"School." He mumbles.

Geez, I don't even know what day it is. The days have been scrambled up with everything going on. "Oh, yes—I forgot."

Sean grunts. He turns in the chair and looks at me with a grim expression. "How can you forgive him so easily, Devon? You know the things he did to me, to Jenn. I know he's my brother and all, but it's so hard to see the man he once was. You know, the good guy."

I understand where Sean's coming from. If all that happened to him, happened to me, I don't know if I could forgive as easily, but I do believe that people deserve second chances. And so far, what I've learned about Jake, he definitely deserves that chance. Especially with learning that Jake did more protecting of Sean than harming him. At least until that last time. "Well, Sean, I won't lie to you. I don't know him like you do. But what I *do* know of him— what I have learned about him—I know he wants a second chance at life. No, wait. I know he *deserves* that second chance. He loves

120

you, Sean. You need to sit down and listen to him, or even just take time and think deep to yourself how you'd feel if the roles were reversed."

Sean nods. A knock on the door has us both look to see who will be walking in. Jenn.

"Hey." Jenn says with her soft voice as she steps around the door. She looks between the two of us. I'm sure she can notice the tension, the frustration we both wear. "Hope I'm not interrupting."

I smile at her. "Not at all. Come sit." I point to the empty chair.

Jenn comes in and walks toward her husband. She kisses him quickly on the lips, and then turns to me. Leaning forward she gives me a quick hug and sits in the empty chair.

"So, what were we talking about?" She asks.

**I had a** great visit with Jenn and Sean. Jenn helps me tag-team Sean on the Jake issue. I hope our point gets across. I really want Jake and his brother to be a family again. Even if it takes time, I want it for them.

Our visit was cut a little short because police officers showed up and wanted to talk. Apparently they wanted to get my statement out of the way so they could get the investigation going. They had a sketch artist with them and I did my best with my descriptions. I told them everything I could remember of the evening, everything leading up to the attack, and what I remember of the actual attack. It was hard to talk about, but I got it done. I'm glad it's over with. I hope the cops catch the bastards.

Now I sit here all alone and wonder what Jake is doing. I hope he isn't upset over the events of this morning. I didn't want to force him out, but I needed that time to talk with Sean. And since it's been hours and Jake hasn't come back, I'm worried. I hope he isn't pissed that I didn't tell him that Sean and I are still friends. I don't want to lose him already, I just found him.

The officer that came to get my statement said that the men I described sounded very familiar to him and that they were well known at the precinct, so it shouldn't be hard to track them down to put them in a line up for me to identify.

With that information a little weight lifts from my chest, knowing that I'll be safe from the assholes that hurt me. But until they're caught, will Jake be safe?

Looking at the clock and the door, my patience wears thin. Where the fuck is he? I don't want to bug him if he is truly busy, but then again I want to know that he is okay. I grab my cell phone of the bedside table and pull up his name from the contact list.

**Where are you?**

I type with my good hand, not wanting to increase the pain levels on my injury.

After what feels like forever, as I stare at my phone for his response, it finally buzzes.

**On my way to you, why? Everything alright?**

I blow out a breath. Thank God he's okay. With those men still on the loose, who knows what can happen?

**Just worried about you.**

I'm not going to lie to him. Keeping secrets or lying will cause more problems than anything at this point, so if I'm honest with him he'll keep true to me, too.

**Just needed a few extra minutes. Almost there.**

Good, he's being honest. But why did he need more time? I sure hope he didn't do anything stupid.

**See you soon.**

Since he's coming, I won't bug him. I set my phone down and try to relax. With the stress of worrying about him, my pain starts to increase. I glance down at my broken, but slowly healing body and see that my dressings are clean. Thankful that all the bleeding has finally stopped and the nurse told me that no infections have presented themselves. I'm hopeful that I'll be able to take the sticky things off soon. I adjust my sling with my uninjured arm and put a pillow underneath. Not wanting another injection for the pain, I ring my buzzer and request from the answering nurse, some acetaminophen.

The nurse just hands me a medicine cup with my pain pills when Jake walks in. His eyes are wary and his body's broody. I don't know what to think, but he sits in the chair beside the bed.

"Thank you." I smile at the nurse and she leaves. I pop the pills in my mouth, reach for my water and swallow down the medicine. I sigh and look to Jake.

"Hey." He says with a small smile. "How are you feeling?"

I stare at him for a moment trying to assess his true mood, but still can't figure it out. I shake my thoughts and smile. "Not bad." I tell him. "The police came in already, so maybe when the doctor comes by she'll let me leave tonight. Well, I hope at least."

Jake perks up. "Oh, what did they say?"

"They have an idea of who the men are, and are pretty sure they can grab them for a line up so I can identify them." Nervousness starts to kick in. I've never been to the police station before to identify anyone for anything. What if my statement doesn't stick? What if the men come after me again because I went to the police? My heart begins to race.

Jake reaches for my hand and grips it tight. "What's wrong, Devon? You look like a scared little girl right now. What just went through your mind?" He stands and moves to sit on the side of the bed.

I look to him, and tears start to well up in my eyes. "What if filing a complaint or charges is a mistake? What if they come after me again?"

Leaning forward, he kisses me right on the lips. His lips are warm and firm on mine and help me shift my thoughts elsewhere.

Pulling back, he moves his hand up and pushes some loose hair out of my face. "Nothing—and I mean nothing will ever happen to you again, Devon. They'll have to go through me to get to you. You're my girl, my life. I protect what's mine." He raises his eyebrows and stares at me, trying to get his point across.

Reaching my arm up, I press it on his chest, gripping his shirt. "I don't want anything to happen to you, either. You mean so much to me, Jake. I never thought I'd find someone to complete me, but I did, and it's you." Tears begin to roll down my cheeks.

# CHAPTER TWENTY-THREE

*Jake*

I wipe the tears that run down her face. Tears that flow because of me. For me. This woman, this angel is my favorite dream come true. I can't let anything happen to her. I won't. I need to get her home and protect her with my life.

"I will be just fine, blondie. I can handle myself." I wipe another random tear and wrap some loose hair behind her ear. I look into her eyes noticing the fear she has, but knowing I'll do everything to squash it.

Devon sniffles and wipes the remainder of her tears. Licking her lips she swallows, and then blows out a breath and frowns. "I don't want you to have to handle yourself. I want us both to be safe. Why can't people just leave us alone?"

Such innocence my girl has. Why did I have to go and ruin her? I'm fucking selfish, that's why. I give her another kiss taking a little more than before. Licking her lips, I demand entrance from her. She submits and I slip my tongue in. I twist and twirl my tongue in her mouth and she returns the actions with hers in fervor. My lips move and devour hers with fierce need and Devon pushes back with equal action. I'm about ready to jump her bones when a voice interrupts us from behind. Fuck.

I pull back immediately, breathing heavy. Devon is flush and I can feel my skin burning up as well. We both look to see who our interruption is. It's Dr. Godwin.

"Sorry to interrupt you both." Dr. Godwin says, embarrassment showing through her body language and the pink color of her skin.

I smirk at her, not trying to be a jerk—but she did just walk in without knocking. "It's okay, doc. What's up?" I ask her.

She shuffles from foot to foot and then looks to Devon. "I heard the police were in today and all your blood work has come back clean. So if you'd like, you can go home tonight. That is if you feel up to it?" She smiles, but her skin is still slightly flushed from the embarrassment.

I look to Devon and she to me. A huge smile forms on her face. I nod to her. Devon smiles and looks back to the doc.

"I feel pretty good and would love to go home." She says.

"I'll have one of the nurses bring in your discharge papers. As for pain medicine, just take some acetaminophen every four to six hours as you need to. Okay?"

Devon nods. "Yes! Thank you so much, Dr. Godwin."

"You're most welcome. Take care of yourself, Devon." She says and walks out.

I feel the bed move and hear Devon's soft voice, but it sounds happier.

"Okay, scoot."

I look at my woman with a grin then chuckle at her. "Scoot?"

She giggles. "Yes. Scoot. Move it. I want out of this bed and out of this hospital."

The sound of her giggle makes my heart thump just a little bit harder. Her smile did a number on me, and now her giggles are doing it. I love every sound she makes. I shake my head at her. "Alright, I'll move, but only for you." But I don't, I just push the chair back a bit to give a little space.

She smiles big and maneuvers herself to the edge of the bed. She's still in a hospital gown, but damn she looks sexy in it. I lick my lips as I take in her bare legs dangling off the side of the bed. Her toes wiggle as if teasing me, tempting me. I browse up her body and when I get to her face she smirks and her eyebrows rise.

Busted! I smile. "Hi." I say, biting my lip.

"Can I help you?" She asks, still smirking.

I shake my head, not knowing what to do. I know I totally just got busted. But what can I do? "No, I think I'm good." I look up and down her delicious body again and hear her laugh.

"I need to get dressed, Jake."

I sigh, knowing I can't just stare at her body all night. "I know. I'm just admiring." I chuckle. I place my hands on her legs, her skin cool to touch. Goosebumps rise as I run my hands slowly up from her knee to her inner thigh. What's wrong with a little teasing on my part? I lick my lips and grin, knowing that I affect her. Moving my hands further, I can feel her legs tremble. Gently, slowly I move further up and slip my hands under the gown. The tops of her thighs are warmer since they were covered by the gown. I glide my fingers across the tops and meet the seam of her underwear. Leaning into her lap, I take a long, deep breath. Instant hard on for me. Fuck. I need to get her home. NOW.

Devon's breath's increase. "Jake, what are you doing? You need to stop."

Yes, I do need to stop. Fuck me, what am I doing? It's just when I'm with her, I can't think with the right brain. "Okay, okay. What can I do to help?" I sit back and adjust my pants.

"Grab my bag from the closet please." She asks with her sweet voice, watching me fix my problem.

I head to the closet that's placed so inconveniently behind the door and grab her backpack. I bring it back to her and set it on the bed. "Anything else, blondie?"

She slowly stands from the bed, taking a moment to get her bearings, grabs the bag and heads to the bathroom. "Nope, I'm going to get dressed. I'll be right back."

"Seriously?" I look to the ceiling and huff out a breath. "Damn you, woman!" I can't believe she is changing in another room after all that. Wait, yes I can. The stupid horny bastard that I am.

There's some slight banging around in the bathroom. Devon must be having troubles getting changed. Bonus for me. "Need help in there?" I shout.

Another bang and a couple grunts, she calls back. "Nope. I got this."

I seem to have lost my touch. Damn. I'll have to see how my luck changes when I get her home. But I'll have to see how her wounds are healing before I start taking advantage of her delicious body.

The nurse comes in while Devon is in the bathroom and hands me the paperwork that has all the details to her discharge and follow-up information. I read through it all, since I plan to take care of my girl. Shit, another two full weeks in that sling. There must be some real damage done there. I try to keep my thoughts calm. My anger wants to rise, thinking of the pain Devon must be in. I clench my eyes shut and a vision of Pike pops up. I'll keep that picture burned in my mind for a later date. If the police don't catch the fucker, then I'll have to find a way to fix things myself.

"Breath, Jake." Devon's sweet voice calls to me.

I didn't know I was holding my breath, anger overcoming me again. I open my eyes and see my girl dressed and ready to leave. "Sorry, blondie." I smile—well, try to. Pike's picture is still fresh and I can't seem to shake it.

"I know you're angry, Jake, but you need to let the police deal with this. You're not that man anymore, remember?" She tips her head and frowns. "We'll get through this. Together." She steps toward me, reaching her hand out…asking me to accept it, to accept her. To move forward with her.

I take her soft hand in my rough one and hold it tight. Standing, I move into her space and wrap her in my arms. She rests her head on my chest and sighs in what I can only assume is content. All my anger disappears with that one sound and I feel better. Kissing the top of her head I ask, "Would you like to walk out or be escorted out by wheelchair?"

She tips her head back and smiles. "Why, escort me, of course." She laughs.

We head to the door and a wheelchair is already waiting outside the room for her. I help her get situated and then push her to the elevator. "You have a prescription for antibiotics with your paperwork. I'll go pick them up after I get you settled." I tell her as we enter the elevator.

She looks up at me and grins. "Sounds good. Now take me home. I've had enough of this place."

JEAN KELSO

# CHAPTER TWENTY-FOUR

*Devon*

We take a cab back to my place. Jake gets me settled on the couch with a cup of hot chocolate and a couple more acetaminophen. He leaves to go pick up my antibiotics, and now I sit here. I could tell that he's still upset over the whole thing. He struggles with trying to be the man he wants to be, and not the man he once was.

I need to prove to Sean that he has changed. I need to prove to Jake that he can change, so I'll do whatever I can to help my man get through this. Knowing that Jenn already forgave him helps. Over the years, Jenn started studying phycology and researching other cases similar to Jake and Sean's. The effects it takes on the children. I think that made it easier for her to forgive. Now for Sean, that'll be another story. But I'm sure with time, they can be brothers again.

Hearing from Jake that I have to wear this damn sling for another two weeks upsets me, but I guess if I want to heal properly I better listen to the doctor. It's not easy using just one hand, one arm, but I'll manage. Plus, I don't think Jake will leave me for long.

I pick up the remote from beside me—where Jake placed it because you know, it's too hard for me to reach for it, silly man—and turn on the television. I need something upbeat, funny to watch. The Bang Theory is on. I love this show. I turn the volume up and prepare myself for a few laughs.

I look at the clock and see it's time to take my pain pills, thankful that Jake set them out. I pick them up along with my mug of now-cold chocolate, but hey—it's chocolate so I'll drink it regardless, and pop the pills in my mouth.

I chug back the rest of my drink and set the mug down. My cell phone rings so I look to see who it is. Jake. I answer. "Hey you, where are you?"

"Just leaving the pharmacy. Are you hungry?" He asks.

I'm silent, thinking when I last ate something. Looking at the clock, it's almost nine in the evening. "I could go for something small, sure."

I hear him chuckle through the phone. "What would you like, Devon?"

I think about the jello and pudding I had in the hospital and think about what I missed most. "Poutine." I nearly shout then laugh. "Sorry—poutine from the diner, please." I tell him.

He laughs again. "And that is something small? Okay. One poutine coming up, blondie. Be there shortly."

I'm still in my yoga pants and tee shirt that I wore home from the hospital. Looking myself over I feel gross, ugly and all the names you can think of, of a girl who hasn't showered in two days. Not knowing how long Jake's going to be I get up off the couch and head to the bathroom.

I relieve myself on the toilet then stand in front the mirror. Bruises still mark my face, but they are starting to fade in darkness. I turn the water on in my shower and begin to strip my pants off—not an easy feat with one arm. Once at my ankles, I kick them aside. Panties, too. I reach up and pull the top part of the sling over my head and ease my arm out, trying not to cause harm to my surgery site.

I set the sling on the vanity and attempt to ease my affected arm through the sleeve of my tee shirt. Once I manage that, I'm able to get the shirt off with no problem. It hurt some, but not as much as if it would've if I hadn't taken my medicine a little while ago.

# JAKE'S REDEMPTION

I look into my mirror and see the bandages. My paperwork said it was safe to remove them when I was ready to shower, so I guess now's the time to do it. One by one, I slowly peel the sticky tape off the edges and lift the bandages off. The marks on my chest are a little red, but don't look too bad, the one on my shoulder is puffy and red and has staples holding it together. I look like a Mrs. Frankenstein. Ugh. How's Jake supposed to be pleased with a body like this? I wipe the tear that leaks from my eye and try to clear my mind. With my arm held against my body, I turn and step under the warm water.

Holy shit, this feels amazing. I'll never take a shower for granted again. The pressure from the water beating down on my scalp, my neck, and my shoulders eases stress and aches I didn't know I had. Steam starts to fill the room and I begin to relax.

I let the water run over my entire body. Reaching for the soap, I take care not to use my affected arm and wash as best as I can. I really wish I could shave, but that'll have to wait for another time. Rinsing off, I grab my shampoo and hold it in my hand. How will I do this? I sure didn't think this through.

Suddenly hard, callused hands rub up my spine. "Hey, baby. Thought you could get naked without me?" Jake's voice's husky and his breath's hot on my neck as he moves closer to me. He takes the shampoo out of my hand. I look over my shoulder at him.

"I wanted to surprise you." I pout.

Jake dumps some shampoo into his hand and puts it in my hair. He begins to massage it onto my scalp and I moan. Damn, that feels glorious.

"Feel good, baby?" He nips my ear.

His body presses against my back. I can feel his erection, hard and ready for action. "It feels like the best thing ever." I moan again as he rubs his hands all over my head, digging his fingers into my scalp.

He kisses my neck, licks where he kisses and runs a trail down my shoulder. He carefully turns me to face him and leisurely licks

133

his way up my neck until he gets to my chin where he nips and then attacks my lips with pure passion. Tipping my head back, he runs his hands over my hair as the water rinses the shampoo out, never releasing my mouth from his pleasuring.

I start to reach my arms up and wince in pain, completely forgetting about my injury. Jake pulls back and takes my hands in his. "No, Devon. Let me." Lust fills his eyes as he sets my arms back down and finishes rinsing my hair.

He leans around me and turns the water off and then grabs us both a towel. He wraps one around his waist and one around my torso. Placing my arm against my body as if it was in the sling he proceeds to pick me up cradle like and steps out of the shower.

"Ah, Jake? What are you doing?" I giggle.

With a huge grin, he walks out of the bathroom and heads to my bedroom. "Taking care of my girl."

In my room, he gently sets me on my bed and opens the towel to expose my body. He climbs onto the bed and crawls over my legs. Staring down at my body, his eyes roam, glistening brightly. His expression unsure, but then he leans down and starts to press little kisses on each of my cuts on my chest. It's as if he's expressing something, but I'm not sure what.

Those cuts are ugly. Why is he kissing them? "Jake? What are you doing?" Tears begin to pool in my eyes. Damn emotions getting the best of me again.

He caresses my arms as he sits and looks at me. "Adoring my beautiful woman."

I sniff. What is he talking about? Beautiful—who's he looking at? "Those are not beautiful." I bite my lip hard to avoid crying out as my own frustration and anger begins to sink in.

Jake wipes the tears from my face. A sincere look, a loving look of compassion stares back at me. "You *are* beautiful, Devon. These marks show survival. You're alive, and to me that's beautiful." He leans down and softly kisses my tear streaked lips, before tracing my surgical cut. "You survived this." His fingers

trail down to the slice on my breast bone. "You survived this."
More tears leak out. His fingers move to just under my breast and
he traces gently across the cut. "You survived this one." I sob. And
finally, he traced the large gash on my stomach. "And you
absolutely survived this one. You're more than beautiful, Devon.
Don't ever think otherwise."

Choking up on my sobs, I try to lighten the mood. I'm not
used to this. "Alright, what have you done with Jake?"

He chuckles lightly and nuzzles his face into my neck. "I'm
right here, blondie. And I'm going nowhere."

Well, damn. This man has done it. My walls are shattered and
I'm in love. Just a couple weeks and he has my heart. I lick my lips
and dry my face with the back of my hand. I stare at him and
memorize every part of his face. I want to remember the moment I
fell completely in my memory forever. "I love you, Jake." I
whisper. I don't expect him to say it back, but I need to express my
feelings.

Jake smiles big, leans down and kisses my nose. "I love you
too, Devon." He crawls off of me and off the bed. Moving to the
dresser he pulls his towel off and pulls some clothes out of the bag
that sits on top.

I'm confused. I thought we were going to have sex. "Uh,
Jake?" I ask.

He turns while pulling up a pair of jogging pants. "Yeah,
blondie?"

I wave my hand up and down my body. "I thought we were
uh… going to uh…"

Opening a drawer, he pulls out a pair of my pajamas. "Sorry,
Devon, but until you are healed a little more there'll be no hanky-
panky."

What? Is he serious? "But I feel okay? Why can't we…?" He
cuts me off mid-sentence.

"Devon, I don't want to hurt you. Until you can go without
taking the pain medicine, I don't want to risk anything. I really am

sorry." He grimaces. "But I'll make up for it when you're better."
He smirks. "For now, I'll help you get dressed. We have some
poutine to eat."

# CHAPTER TWENTY-FIVE

*Jake*

It's been three days since I brought Devon home from the hospital. The police still haven't called to give any updates, and Devon has started to have nightmares again. She says she'll be okay, that they're not as bad as I think they are—but I don't believe her. I think she's hiding her feelings to prevent me from getting angry.

The more time that goes by with no arrest, the further on edge I become. Who's to say Pike and his men aren't going to come after Devon again? I think I'm going to get Sean's phone number from Devon, and see if he'll meet with me. I need to know if he knows anything about Dom's whereabouts. Dom may be a criminal, but he too is our brother and that should come first. At least it used to. He too used to be a good man and stood up for me when the times were right…well, when he was around. I have no idea why his lackeys are being pricks—with the exception of the trial, but it's been years.

I'm at the diner now picking up some lunch for us. Devon's off work until the sling comes off, or until the doctor gives the go-ahead to return. She hasn't wanted to leave the house these past few days, so I've been doing the running around. I understand her fear, but I can't let her stay holed up indoors forever.

"Hey, Jake. Here's your order." Mark sets a paper bag down on the counter and leans on his elbows. "How's our girl doing?" He asks.

Over the past few days, Mark and I have gotten to know each other. He knows I'm going nowhere. He knows my feelings for Devon are genuine and that I'll do anything to protect her. "Well, man, she's not doing that great. The pain's better and she's healing physically, but she won't leave the house." I pull out my wallet and grab two twenty's to pay him. "I think I may have to force her out. She needs a change of scenery. And she has nightmares. I just hope she can get over this."

Mark nods and stands. "She's a tough girl. She'll get through it. And with you by her side. She can do it." He smacks his hand on the counter and smiles. "Anyways, say hi to my baby girl and you take care, you hear?"

I nod, grab the takeout bag and head out the door.

Five minutes or so from the diner a car drives up really slow. It puts me on alert. I watch as it comes up and the window goes down. An arm sticks out and a gun flashes in the sun. Immediately, I follow the arm up to the face and I see Pike with a grin. As if everything is in slow motion, the gun fires and I dive toward the ground. I'm too slow. Instant burning fire runs down my arm. Screams surround me and tires squeal as the car takes off.

I'm a little dizzy, but I roll to my back and take deep breaths. Turning my head, I look around to make sure everyone around is alright. People run about, yelling to call nine-one-one. I hear footsteps come close and Mark's in my face.

"Fuck, Jake! Are you hit?" Mark looks me over.

Feeling the pain radiate from my upper arm to my tingling fingers, I nod. I sit up and look at my arm to assess it. Blood rushes out and pours down. "Shit. Yeah, I was." I wrap my hand around it and look to Mark. "Was anyone else hit?"

Mark shakes his head. "No. Everyone is just panicked." He helps me stand up and I stumble. My take out bag is ripped and lunch is scattered on the sidewalk. Well, damn it. So much for having lunch.

"I called for an ambulance already." Mark says. Sirens already can be heard in the distance. "Do you know who it was?" He asks.

"Fuck yeah, I do. It's the fucker that hurt Devon." I growl.

"Shit, Devon. Should I call her?" Mark raises his eyebrows.

I shake my head. "Sure. Check on her. Let her know that there was a situation and you're just checking in. But please don't tell her about me. I'll let the paramedics check me out then head home to her." Anger wavers under my skin. The beast in me wants out— wanting to kill the fucker who dare come after me. Who dare hurt my woman.

It's getting harder to be the better man when shit like this keeps happening. My damn past needs back the fuck off and stay in the past. Why can't I have a new life? A happy life? Fuck!

The ambulance arrives along with a police cruiser. I sit in the ambulance as they assess, clean and wrap up my bullet wound. It's just a deep flesh wound, so it isn't too bad. It bleeds like a sucker, but I refuse to go to the hospital. The police grill me about the incident and I tell them about Devon's situation and to look into that. That it's the same men for both scenarios.

With my wound dealt with, my statement taken and the crowd now under control, I'm back at the diner waiting to get more lunch.

"Maybe you and Devon should stay somewhere different until they catch those guys. Somewhere safer?" Mark says when he hands me another bag of takeout.

"I'll talk with her, but I don't know if she'll agree with it. I might talk to my brother and see if he can help. But thanks, Mark." I shake his hand, grab lunch and leave again. Hopefully, I can make it back home in one piece.

I walk into Devon's. She sits on the couch watching television. She looks at me and immediately her smile goes into a look of alarm. "What happened?" She jumps up from the couch with a wince and comes to me.

I keep walking in until I reach the dining area and set the paper bag on the table. "I'm okay, Devon. Calm down." I sit in a chair and begin to open the bag of food.

She sits in the chair across from me. "That doesn't explain what the fuck happened. Jake? Please don't hide things from me." Fear is strong in her voice.

I don't want to scare her, but she's right. I can't keep it from her. "Pike's still around. He did a drive by, but missed his target you could say."

She pounces up and begins to pace the area. "Missed? There's blood on your shirt. How's that a miss?"

I set the food aside, stand and stop Devon in her tracks. I wrap her in my arms and hold her tight. "Shh, baby. It's alright. It's a flesh wound. I'm okay. The police know what happened and will call when they find anything."

I feel her body shake and just know that she's crying. I don't know how else to calm her. My poor woman has been enduring more than she needs to. "Maybe we should stay someplace else for a while?" I tell her.

She peeks up at me and sniffs. "No. I won't leave my home. We'll get an alarm." She licks her lips and frowns. "We can't let him win."

I understand what she's saying. We need to stand and show no fear. He can't break us. But we can't do it alone. "I need to call Sean."

"You can use my phone." She steps out of my embrace and heads to the table. "What's for lunch?" She asks.

Leave it to food to sidetrack her. I laugh to myself. "Cheeseburgers and chili fries."

"Oh, yummy." She whips open her platter and picks at a fry.

"Are you going to be okay, Devon?" I ask her. I know between her emotional outbreaks and the fear, I don't think she knows if she is coming or going—but I don't want her to think that she's weak.

"Yeah, I will be. Sorry. Bet you don't think I'm still beautiful with all these messed up moods, eh?" She laughs.

I march up to her, grasp her face in my hands and press my lips to hers. I plunge my tongue deep into her mouth and search her out. She moans. Sucking her lip into my mouth, I tease. Nipping and nibbling, I inhale her moans and groan in return.

Pulling back, I stare her down. "You're beautiful all the time. When you're crying, when you're yelling, when you're happy and even when you don't know what mood you're in. Never doubt it, baby." Another peck to her lips, I go to the coffee table and snag her cell phone. "You dig in, I'm calling Sean."

With a mouth full of fries, she mumbles. "Ookkaay."

I shake my head at her. What a woman.

I scroll through her contact list and find Sean. Hitting dial I wait. It rings. Once. Twice. He picks up. "Hey, Devon, how are you?"

"It's Jake. Sorry to bother you." I tell him, hoping he isn't pissed that it's me on the phone.

"Oh…hey, Jake. Is Devon okay?" He asks. He doesn't sound angry, so that's a good sign.

I sit on the couch and lean on my knees. "She's doing better."

"Good, good."

"Here's the thing, Sean. The guys that beat up Devon did a drive by today on me."

"They what?" Sean's voice rising.

"Yeah, the police haven't caught them yet and I guess they're still out for me. I have a flesh wound, but it's okay. I need to find Dom. They're his lackeys."

A long breath blows out on the other end. "Damn, man. I don't know how to get a hold of him. When everything was done with court and the search went on for him, he wasn't found. The last I heard, he made his way up to Canada somewhere. I haven't heard from him, either."

I scratch my head and then rest my hand on the back of my neck. "Serious? Canada?"

"Why don't you just take care of it?" Sean asks with a bit more attitude in his voice.

I knew it'd be hard to have a normal chat with him, but at least it started off normal. "Sean, I'm not that man anymore. I don't want to be that man. Can't you help me out here? Understand that?" I sigh.

"Ah, fuck man. I'm trying. This isn't easy. You were a jackass for years, remember?"

"Yeah, I do. But I never actually hurt you, or meant to. I want to fix that. I want to be your brother again. I want to be a better man. Can you help with that?" What else can I say to him? I do want his help. I want his help with everything. I can't do it alone. I want my brother back.

"I'll do my best, Jake. Just remember, lay a finger on Jenn or my daughter and I *will* fucking kill you." Sean says rather bluntly.

"I got you." I tell him. I really want him to understand that.

"Alright. I do have a connection or two in Canada that I can use to try and track Dom. I'll see if I can get a message to him for you. We good?" He asks.

"That would rock. Thanks, Sean." I blow out a breath, look over my shoulder at Devon as she bites down on her cheeseburger. Ketchup drips down her chin. I chuckle to myself.

"Don't thank me yet. There's no guarantee that the message will get to him. But I'll try."

"That's all I ask."

"Later, Jake."

"Later, Sean." I hang up and go and sit with Devon. She's half way done her food and has a big smile on her face.

"This is so good." She mumbles.

# CHAPTER TWENTY-SIX

### *Devon*

It's been a long two weeks and I'm going to the doctors today. I want the all clear to go back to work. I want Jake to stop babying me and fuck me already. I'm so damn horny and I want him balls deep inside of me tonight. All the teasing he has been doing with the kisses, nips and nibbles have driven me right up the wall. I actually dreamt about jumping him in his sleep, but even in my dreams, he stopped me—stupid man.

Jake's doing some running around, getting new locks for the windows on the house and picking up groceries. So I'm at the doctors by myself. I think he just doesn't want to see them remove the staples and stitches. Sometimes I think men just act tough.

The receptionist calls my name and I set the magazine down that I have to head in her direction. She puts me in a room and tells me the doctor will be right with me.

Not even ten minutes later Dr. Godwin walks in and shuts the door behind her. "Hello, Devon. How are you?" She asks with a smile.

I wasn't expecting to see her again, but it's nice to have the same doctor who operated on me.

"I'm doing wonderful, doc. I'm ready for everything to be back to normal now." I laugh.

"I bet you are." She moves in front of me and begins to remove the sling. "Can we remove the shirt?"

I take it off with no problems. "Everything feels great." I tell her.

She reaches into the box of gloves on the treatment table and pulls a pair out. Slipping them on she begins to assess my now practically healed wounds. "These all look great. Let's get the stitches and staples out, shall we?"

I nod with agreement. "Yes please."

Dr. Godwin walks over to a cupboard and takes out a sterile wrapped tray and brings it over to the table beside me. Back over at the cupboard she takes out a bottle of clear fluid and brings it back over. Opening the tray, she pulls out a pair of little scissors and a mini staple remover thing. She opens the fluid and dumps it in a little bowl. She changes her gloves and proceeds to clean my wounds then removes the stitches and staples. I don't bleed so bandages aren't needed.

"Well, that should do it." She says. "No infection is present. You're good to go." She smiles.

"That's great. So can I go back to work?"

"Oh yes. You can resume everything you were doing before."

"Everything?" I ask openly with a smirk.

Dr. Godwin laughs. "Yes, Devon—you're able to do that, too."

"Woohoo. If he says no now, I'll kick his ass."

The doc laughs a full belly laugh. "Oh, my! You're hilarious. Go get him, tiger."

**I get home** and Jake isn't home yet. I hop in the shower and shave. I've been waiting two long weeks to have his body entangled with mine and I'm not waiting any longer. I soap up head to toe, shampoo, and conditioner. I dry off and rush to my room. Digging through my drawers, I find a lacey, red camisole and a matching thong. An idea pops into my head. I put the lingerie on and head to my closet for heels. Finding a nice sleek black pair, I put them on. Back to the bathroom I style my hair and put on some makeup.

I don't know when Jake will be back, but I want to be ready. I head to the living room and gear up the stereo with some music, pour myself a glass of white wine, and lounge on the couch. I position myself in a pose as seductive as I can and wait.

Geez, men are slow. I'm on my second glass of wine. I just get resettled back on the couch when the door opens. It takes a minute for Jake to notice me. But when he does, he drops the bags he carries.

"Fuck me, you're hot." He licks his lips and steps forward, bags all but forgotten.

I run my hand up my exposed stomach and bite my lip. "You like?" I ask.

"Like? I fucking love it." He growls.

He's about to pounce on me, but I shout. "No!"

He stops dead in his tracks. "Wait. What?"

I pick up my wine, chug back the remains and slam it down on the table. "You, bedroom, naked, now." I point and smirk.

He raises his eyebrows and grins. "Oh, blondie. Are you going to stoke a fire?"

I begin to sit up on the couch. "If you don't get moving, there will be no fire for you. Now move it."

I have never seen a man move so fast in my life. I close my eyes tight. This is going to be fun. So much fun.

I take my time getting to the bedroom, stopping in the doorway taking in the scenery. Jake is sprawled on the bed, naked and waiting. His muscles are hard and tense, patience being held by a thread.

"I got the all clear from the doctor today." I tell him trying to sound sexy, but I'm sure it didn't sound it.

"Oh, yeah?" His eyes narrow as he browses my body from head to toe.

"Yeah. And you've been a very bad boy by denying me pleasure over the past two weeks." I narrow my eyes at him and begin to walk towards him.

145

He grips his cock and begins to stroke it. "Have I, really?"

The sight of him pleasuring himself gives me tingles between my legs. I need him now. I get to the end of the bed and start to crawl on. "Yes, you have. And for that, I believe I deserve…let's see…" I glide my hand up his calf and then my other hand glides up his other leg. "Two orgasms." Moving my hands up further.

His body shivers and I feel it. It urges me on with my teasing.

"Just two?" He asks as he strokes his now massively hard cock.

I think momentarily. "Maybe three." I slide my body up his until I'm straddling him. He's still stroking and I'm watching. Biting my lip, I debate on taking over. But I don't. I lean over him and press warm kisses to his bare chest. I tease his nipples, taking one in my mouth, sucking and biting lightly. Listening to him groan, I move to the other I repeat my actions.

I lick my way up his chest—his neck, his chin, then his mouth. I dip my tongue inside and let the battle of the sexes begin.

His tongue fights me every twist, every turn. I nip his lip, he nips back. Heat begins to rise and tingles flow through me.

"Devon." He mumbles between kisses.

"Jake."

I feel his hand between my legs, pushing the fabric of my thong aside and I moan. He swipes his fingers back and forth, wetness increases and he dips two fingers inside. "Ohhh…" I moan loudly.

He pushes them in and out—and it feels magnificent. I push back on his fingers wanting more. I even tell him, "More. Jake, I want more."

In a flash, I'm on my back. Jake sucks my ear lobe. It drives me nuts. I've always had a thing with my ears. Wowza. Butterflies swim in my stomach. He bites and licks while fire burns everywhere in me.

With my thong pushed aside, he presses his cock against my pussy and rubs it back and forth. "God, Devon. I've been waiting for this for two weeks." He slowly starts to push in and I begin to melt. It feels so good. He pushes more and pulls back. Pushes again and groans. "Fuck."

"Don't stop." I growl.

He chuckles. "Oh, I don't plan to." He pulls back and pushes back in harder and faster—and damn it feels amazing. I close my eyes and let the sensations take me.

I wrap my legs around his waist and lift my hips.

He pumps and thrusts, harder, faster and grinds our pelvis's together. My clit's on fire. I'm ready to scream, but I wait. "Jake. Jake. Oh, God. Hurry." I pant.

He thrusts faster and I dig my nails into his back. He leans down, sucks a nipple into his mouth through the lacey fabric, and bites down. I'm done for. My whole body starts to convulse and spasm around him. "Jake…" I groan loudly as my body shakes uncontrollably.

Jake thrusts two more times and groans out his release. With sweat trickling down his face, he tucks his face into my neck. "God—I love you, Devon."

He collapses down onto the bed and rolls to his side. We both breathe heavy, but I feel better—that's for sure.

"Thank you." I say for no reason.

Jake chuckles. "You're more than welcome, baby."

I smile. "I really needed that. Don't ever make me wait that long again."

"Yes, ma'am." He wraps an arm around my waist and kisses my shoulder.

JEAN KELSO

# CHAPTER TWENTY-SEVEN

*Jake*

I leave Devon satiated and naked in bed to shower after round three. Once I'm dressed I head to the living room to grab my phone. Seeing a notification, I check my messages. There's one from Sean. I sure fucking hope this is good news. Keying in my password, I unlock it and read the message.

**My source says he gave word to his sources, and that word will be sent to Dominic about the situation.**

I grimace in thought. That's a lot of sources. Shaking my head, I chuckle. But I guess that's better than nothing...but how's that helping us now?

**When will we know if he is going to help?**

I type out and wait. Immediately Sean responds.

**Sources say shouldn't be long.**

Hmmph...well, I guess I'll have to sit on my hands and wait then. I never used to do that, but I don't want to drag Devon down any further than I already have. I'd rather die than have her hurt again.

**Alright, thanks, man.**

I set my phone down and go to the kitchen to make some coffee. Devon should need a caffeine fix soon. I'm sure she want rounds four, five, and possibly six anytime. I smirk to myself. Well, I know I do. I can't get enough of her.

My phone buzzes again. Finishing up and turning the coffee on, I go and pick up my phone. It's another message from Sean.

**Stay safe, brother.**

Well, shit. My heart beat a little harder. He cares…well, he must at least care a little to say that. Progress is being made. That makes me feel just a little stronger, better about our bond healing.

**You too, bro.**

I text back and set my phone back down to head toward the bedroom. It's getting close to dinner time and I'm starved. I need to see what my girl wants to eat.

I stand in the doorway of the bedroom. Devon is still naked, laying on the bed with a sheet just covering her gorgeous body from the waist down. She lies on her stomach with one leg slightly bent. Her head's curled up on a pillow with an arm tucked underneath. She looks like an angel laying there. Beautiful. And she's mine. I sigh. Looking up, I close my eyes and smile. I send a little prayer to the heavens. "Thank you." I whisper to the man above.

I don't want to disturb her, but it's time to wake my girl. She needs sustenance and I need her.

At the bottom of the bed, I grip the sheet and slowly begin to pull it off of her. The soft cloth glides down her soft skin inch by inch exposing her body to me, delighting me with the gift God gave me. I grin. Devon doesn't stir as the material falls off, exposing her nakedness.

Moving around the bed, I lean over her and gently move some hair away from her face, and kiss her forehead. "Time to wake up, blondie." I whisper softly.

Devon still doesn't move. I place my hand on her upper back and caress it slowly down her spine. The hairs on her neck rise and I smile. Finally, a reaction. I twirl my fingers in a circle at the base of her spine and move to her ass. Her breath hitches and a thought comes to mind.

"You feel me, baby?" I whisper in her ear then begin to nibble on her lobe.

Devon moans. My girl is waking up. I squeeze her ass, and then give it a quick smack.

"Ahh…" Devon's eyes open in a flash and she looks to me. "That was mean."

Smirking, I lean further in and kiss her on the lips. "Well, you were taking so long to wake up. I had to do something, baby."

She starts to roll over so I move to allow her space. Lying on her back, her perky breast now fully exposed to me, I can't help but look and take in her pure beauty. Damn, I'm one lucky fucker. I stare for longer than I should, but I can't help myself.

"Jake, is everything okay?" Devon asks as she starts to sit up.

Immediately my gaze moves up to her face and I smile. "Yeah, I'm great, blondie. Sorry. I was struck with your beauty and couldn't drag my eyes away."

She blushes and the color looks gorgeous on her. Just that touch of pink on her cheeks is perfect. No makeup is needed for my girl. The natural look is all she needs.

Looking her up and down one more time I clear my thoughts of the naughty ones that are sitting in the front of my mind. "What would you like to eat for dinner?" I ask her.

Devon bites her lip, and then smiles. "Pizza." She tells me and moves to get out of the bed.

"Homemade or order in?" I raise my eyebrow. I'm good with either, but I will do whatever my girl wants.

She runs her fingers through her hair trying to fix her sexy bed head. "Take out, please."

I stop in the doorway and look at my girl one last time before leaving to order dinner. I shake my head. "Beautiful. Just beautiful."

Devon blushes again and I walk out to get dinner sorted.

I ordered a large pepperoni, bacon with extra cheese for us, that way there would be left over for us to snack on. I heard the shower turn off a few minutes ago, so Devon should be coming out to me soon.

I grab a mug from the cupboard and put the fixings for her coffee in the mug. Her soft pitter-patter of footsteps comes up behind me as I pour the coffee in. Bare arms wrap around my waist as I set the pot of hot liquid down. Smiling to myself, I turn in said arms and wrap my arms around her shoulders.

"Hey, blondie, feel better?"

She sets her chin on my chest and is smiling. "I feel great. With great sex, a nice nap, and a hot shower, why shouldn't I feel this good?" Devon winks and stares at me.

My girls in a playful mood. She has a little kinky side. I like it. I think I like it a lot. "Great sex you say?" I smirk as I look down at her.

She sticks her tongue between her teeth in a playful way as she smirks. And I think it's the most adorable look ever. "The best sex ever. From the sexiest man on the planet." She giggles.

Oh, she's being a bad girl now. "Oh, so you think you're funny now?" I move one arm and reach down to smack her ass. My other arm moves right after, grabbing her ass and pulling her closer to me. "Is the funny girl looking for trouble?"

Devon squeaks as she tucks her face closer to my chest. "I haven't had…" She mumbles.

I reach my hand up and lift her face with my fingers. "I didn't hear that, blondie. Look at me when you talk." I narrow my eyes at her, her skin flushes pink as I stare at her.

Her breathing increases.

I wait patiently for her to tell me. I don't want to push her. She actually seems nervous, shy at saying what's on her mind. Which seems odd considering she lets me see her naked. But everyone has sides to their personality, right? I definitely won't push.

After blowing out a soft breath she whispers clearly, loud enough for me to hear. "I haven't had my fill of you, yet." Her lip disappears. I know she bites it. It must be a nervous habit, but damn if it doesn't turn me on.

I bend my knees slightly, pull Devon closer and grind my hard cock against her. I'll never be done with her, either. I have a void that has her name on it, and I don't think it'll ever fill. "Do you feel that, Devon?" I ask as I rub along her pelvis.

Her eyes close for a moment then she looks at me and nods. "Yes."

I lean closer, get face to face with her. Her warm breath blowing against me, I take in her scent. "I'm not done with you either." I kiss her lips hard then pull back. "But we're eating some dinner before play time begins.

I must be hitting her clit as I rub. Devon's body shivers when it hits that spot each time. Proud of myself, I grind a few more times before I kiss her on the nose and turn to grab her coffee.

"Here's some caffeine." I grin a huge grin to show her I mean play business.

She takes the mug and heads toward the living room. I take out another mug and make a drink for myself before heading out to sit with her.

I flick on the television and find a show to numb our minds and the doorbell goes off.

"Yay, food." Devon says.

I chuckle as I get up to get the door. Pulling my wallet out of my pocket I open the door. I greet the delivery kid—who doesn't even look old enough to drive the beat up truck I see parked out front over his shoulder. He hands me the box of cheesy deliciousness and I hand him a twenty. After telling him to keep the change, I close the door and bring the pizza to the kitchen.

"Fork and knife, blondie?" I call to her from the kitchen.

"Naw, just on a plate with some napkins please." She shouts back.

I grab plates, napkins, and the pizza and bring it all back to the living room. Setting it all on the coffee table, I ask. "One or two?" I open the box and start to put a slice on a plate.

"One for now." She says.

I hand her a plate, pile my plate with two, and sit back. The television is on low, which is fine with me. I had put on some random show and Devon hadn't complained. Looking at the screen now, I'm wondering if I even read the name of the show.

Monkeys. Monkeys are everywhere. In the trees. On rocks. Monkeys are screwing too. I look to Devon and she is watching the show. What the hell? "Uh, blondie?" I ask and she looks to me.

"Yeah, Jake?"

I point to her and then to the television. "What the hell are you watching?" I don't want to sound like a complete idiot. I know there are monkeys, but seriously.

"Monkeys." She simply says and turns to watch the show again.

Yep, I'm an idiot. I watch her for a minute then look back at my plate. Whatever. Picking up a slice I dig in. And damn, it is good. Taking another bite, I look up and get suckered into watching the furry-fuckers fuck some more.

This is nuts. I think I have lost at least ten brain cells watching this. I set my empty plate on the table and sit back. Looking over at Devon, I stare, stupefied. Feeling stupid from watching the show and terrified for the fact that Devon liked. I guess that is the difference between people when they talk interests. Is it an educational show? I don't know. Shit, I just learned something. But still, I need to know.

"Seriously?" I blurt.

Devon looks at me, crossing her legs on the couch, having already finished her dinner, plate on the table.

"About what?"

Now she really must be joking. I point to the plasma box in the corner. "That!" I exclaim. "How can you sit through half an hour of monkeys fucking?" I twist my body to face her, proving I mean how serious I am.

Devon slouches and puts her hands in her lap, her expression is saying that I'm an idiot. It tells me, that she thinks I should know this. Like, come on already. "It's just nature, Jake. Plus, monkeys are cute." Her head tilts and she grins, her point presenting itself clearly.

How could I have not known? Fuck. I'm just a man, right?

"Oh, I'm sorry. How could I not know?" I say sarcastically.

Devon moves forward onto her hands and knees, crawling toward me. "It's primal, Jake. Sexy." Her hands move up my body and then she straddles my lap. "Sex. It turns me on, Jake." She looks into my eyes, looking so serious, but something is hiding there.

Glaring, her eyes glisten. Holy shit, monkey sex made her horny? My eyes pop and I press myself back against the couch.

# JEAN KELSO

# CHAPTER TWENTY-EIGHT

*Devon*

Oh my God, look at his eyes. He believes me. Shit. I'm trying to stay in the playful mood, not scare the shit out of him. I start to laugh, show that I'm joking. Fuck, I hope this works. "No, no, Jake. I'm kidding. Joking with you." This isn't going the way I wanted it to go.

Jake still stares. I put both of my hands on the sides of his face. "Jake, look at me." Fuck, I freaked him out. "I'm kidding." Feeling like crap for my joke not working out, I begin to move off of him, but his hands are on me as soon as I shift.

"Where are you going?" His expression of shock is gone. The look he shows is new, dark, intriguing. The beast is here, time to play.

I stop moving and look at him. His eyes have darkened and his lids are hooded. It's a naughty look, sexy. I love it. A tingle in my belly and I know I'm ready. "To bed?" I raise my eyebrows and bite my lip. I know he loves that.

Jake grips me tight and turns on the couch. We are up and I wrap my legs fully around his waist. My arms around his neck, I look at him with a smile.

Jake's eyes glisten with mischief and the thought of it excites me.

"To bed we go then, blondie. You're in trouble anyways." He looks at me with an evil grin and my heart begins to race.

"Am I going to get punished?" I ask, feeling hopeful for a spanking or two. I'm not into the major kinky stuff, but since the first time Jake spanked me, I have enjoyed the odd one.

He licks his lips and waggles his eyebrows. "Oh baby, you sure are." He walks right into the bedroom and tosses me on the bed.

**Waking up the** next morning, I'm stiff and sore—but in all the right places. My punishment wasn't necessarily punishment at all. I enjoyed every minute of it. Jake seems to know how to play my body like a well-known instrument, making it hum and sing with just the right touch. Just thinking about it has me smiling.

I look over to the side of the bed, but it's empty. Jake seems to be an early riser—which I don't mind—but waking in his arms is like a dream and I love it.

Getting out of bed, I toss on a pair of sleep boxers and a tank top. Then I head out to the living room in search of my man.

Jake's in the kitchen where the smell of bacon makes me moan. He looks so sexy standing at my stove in just a pair of jeans hanging low at his waist. He's barefoot, and looks good enough that I'm willing to ignore the bacon and take him back to bed with me.

He turns as I enter the kitchen, turning the stove off as he does with a smile, big and beautiful on his face. "Morning, blondie. I made breakfast." He starts to dish out bacon onto the plate he has set beside the stove, eggs and toast already laid out.

I get close and wrap my arms around his waist. My cheek to his chest, absorbing his smell, I peek up at him. "Looks delicious. Maybe I'll call Mark and tell him I still don't feel good and I'll skip out on work today." I give him the puppy eyes. The way he treats me is amazing. I could stay home all day and feel loved like this. I don't ever want to let go.

With a kiss to my nose and smack to my ass, he grins. "As nice as that would be, blondie, you're not missing your first day back."

I pout. I know he's right. I do love my job, my customers and of course, Mark. But I want more of Jake. More of last night. Damn, I'm turning into a sex addict. Who would have thought?

Unwrapping my arms, I step back and take the plate full of yummy looking food and head to my dining table. I look over my shoulder, still pouting. "I know. But you better be here when I get home." I turn my pout around and give him a sexy smirk. I hope he understands what I mean by it. If not, I'll need to learn how to do this sexy shit for him.

Jake fixes himself a plate and comes to sit with me. His smile hasn't changed, so I don't know if he got my point or not. Silence fills the room, and I start to eat.

"Oh, fuck—these are good." I groan. The eggs are the best I have ever had. I look to Jake with wonder. He can cook. Sexy, great in bed and he cooks. I scored with this man.

"I know." He grins hugely.

Oh! He's cocky, too—the bastard. Well then, I guess I'll let him have that one. My time will come. I laugh and keep eating. I guess he isn't going to tell me the secret, and I'm not going to ask. Stupid man.

I swallow my last bite and look at the clock. With less than an hour left to get to work, I guess I should get ready. I pick up my plate and bring it to the kitchen. "I need to get ready for work. What are your plans for the day, Jake?"

We pass each other in the kitchen doorway. He puts his plate in the sink and turns to me. "Walk you to work. Then I really don't have any plans." He shrugs.

"Well, you can hang at the diner for a little. I'm sure Mark won't mind. But you can't stay the whole shift unless you work there." Well, shit. Why didn't I think of that? I'll ask Mark to give Jake a job. I'm sure there's something he could help with.

With that thought in mind, I head to the bathroom to shower and get ready for work.

I'm standing in my bedroom, looking in the mirror. So far I have my bra and underwear on. All my scars are noticeable, but things are healed. What I went through has affected me in so many ways, but Jake doesn't see it the way I do. He still sees me as beautiful. It will be a very long time before I see what he does. Sometimes for work, I wear crop shirts and short shorts, but I think I won't be wearing those for a while. It gets warm in the diner, but I won't show my scars. Not yet.

I open my bottom drawer and pull out a pair of loose fitting jeans, faded blue. Opening the drawer above it I pick through my selection and decide on a tee shirt that covers my full torso. I like to have something to let customers chat about, so I pick a shirt that says *book boyfriends do it better*. I know for sure someone will make a comment or two about it. I'm sure Jake will. I snicker to myself as I start to pull it over my head.

I pull my jeans on, grab a belt from my closet and put on a pair of socks. Looking in the mirror again I see that I'm fully covered and feel good about it.

The bruises have faded to a very light yellow on my face, so just a dab of cover up will help conceal those. I apply a layer of it and brush my hair. A final once over in the mirror and I'm good to go.

Heading out to the living room, Jake is already dressed with his shoes on, sitting on the couch waiting for me. Looking to me as I walk in the room he looks me over and smiles. "You look good."

He knows not to complain or cause a fuss, another plus. Yeah, I think I'll keep him. "Thanks. I'm ready when you are." I tell him and head to the door to put my shoes on. I decide sneakers would work best being my first day back if I have any lingering aches, I don't want to be wearing heels to inflict further pain.

Walking into the diner a shiver runs up my spine. It's the first time I've been here since the attack. I stop at the bar, Jake stops with me, and I look around. Everything is back in its place. No blood anywhere, no broken glass on the floor, nothing. It's like nothing happened. But I know the truth. I take a deep breath. Fear from the memories rising. Jake puts his hand on my shoulder and I look at him.

"I'm right here. You are safe, Devon." He looks into my eyes. Into my soul. The reassurance is deep and I can feel it. I nod at him and breath again. I can do this.

I look around again and notice familiar faces. Sean, Jenn, and little Sofie are here. They are sitting in a corner booth and are looking my way. Mark must have told them I'm returning to work today. Them being here for support sure feels good. I can't help but smile at them. Little Sofie waves at me and I wave back.

# JEAN KELSO

# CHAPTER TWENTY-NINE

*Jake*

Devon smiles. That's a good sign. Who's she waving to? I follow her gaze and complete awe strikes. A little blonde girl waves back. The spitting image of my mother in child form sits in a booth at this very diner. My heart starts to race. My chest feels tight. Such a beautiful little girl. I feel Devon's hand on my arm, so I break my gaze and look to her. She's smiling still.

"Beautiful isn't she?"

I look back to the girl, lost in my own little dream world. Fuck yeah, she is. "Who…" I start to ask.

"Jake." I hear a familiar voice call. I'm shaken from my daze and focus on the woman calling to me. It's Jenn. Sean is with her. That means the little girl is my niece, Sofie. Holy shit. Panic starts to fill me.

Devon's warm breath is on my face and her hands squeeze my arm. "You have this, Jake. Go meet your niece." She whispers in my ear and kisses my cheek. She walks away and I take a deep breath.

Can this actually be happening? Sofie—my niece—sits just feet in front of me. She looks just like our mother. I loved our mom and our dad murdered her. It's hard to shake the shock. But fuck, if Devon can return to a place where she was traumatized, then I can do this. I take another deep breath and head toward my family. Family, fuck that feels good to say.

I stop when I get to the booth and take in my brother and his wife. They're a good looking couple, that's for sure. Looking at little Sofie, I can't help but stare. Her eyes, the hair, her tiny little nose. All I see is mom.

"Have a seat, Jake." Jenn points to the empty spot beside Sean. I nod and sit, still staring at Sofie.

"Dude, stop staring at her." Sean grumbles. I flick my head and look at him, a smirk now present. "She doesn't need a complex." He shakes his head. I hear Jenn giggle.

"She's beautiful, man."

"Thanks."

"Spitting image…"

"Of mom, I know." Sean looks at his daughter, I follow his look and Sofie looks at us both. So innocent and young. And I missed out on the start of her life. Well, sure hope I don't miss out on more.

"Hi, Uncle Jake." Her sweet little voice flows across the table to me and my heart thumps harder. They told her about me. Fuck that feels even better. Is it possible to fall in love instantly? Because her little voice saying hi to me, is all it took. I love this little girl already.

"Hey, Sofie." I can feel tears start to pool in my tear ducts, I fight them. I don't want to look like a big wuss. I want to be a cool uncle. "It's awesome to meet you."

Sofie smiles big and takes a sip of her chocolate milk.


**I sit at** the bar. Devon said she was going to stop and have a quick break with me before I leave. I had an amazing visit with Sean, Jenn, and little Sofie and I feel so alive right now. Things are looking up for me, for sure. I have an amazing woman. I have my brother back for the most part. I have a beautiful niece that I plan to spoil the shit out of. What more could I ask for? This is a great new life. A new start's what I wanted and I definitely love it.

I'm sipping on my coffee when Devon slides onto the stool beside me. "Hey."

I turn to face her and smile. "Hey back, blondie." I set my mug down and lean in for a kiss. I get a quick but satisfying one and sit back. "How is the shift going?" I ask.

She looks around the diner and back to me. "Pretty good. No pain so far." She reaches for my mug and steals a sip.

I laugh at her for being sneaky, but heck, I love the woman, she can steal whatever she wants from me. "Good to hear."

She starts to pick at her shirt and nibbling on her bottom lip. "So, I talked to Mark for a few minutes while I was waiting for an order."

Well, if the way she said that wasn't mysterious, I don't know what is. "Okay. What did you talk about?" I raise my eyebrows. She obviously wants me to know, or she wouldn't have mentioned it.

She blows out a quick breath and slaps a hand on the counter. "Okay! If you want a job, Mark said you can work here." She blurts out.

Stunned with what she said I look to the order window of the kitchen and back to her. "Say what?"

"A job, Jake."

I'm confused. I never once complained about not having a job. Yeah, sure I'm looking, but she doesn't have to ask for favors to get me one. "Devon, baby, you didn't have to do that." I pull her closer, almost off her stool.

"I know Jake, but this way we can both have something to do. Make some money, and you won't have to worry about me all the time." She bites her lip, hope written all over her face.

I've never thought of all that. She makes good points. I suppose I could handle working at the diner, wiping tables, doing some dishes and other shit, if it makes her happy. At least until something better comes up, and especially until we are out of danger. "Okay, blondie. I'll do it." I poke her nose in teasing, then lean in and kiss her warm lips.

"Awesomesauce." She stands from her stool and gives me a huge hug. "I'll let Mark know you said yes,and then I need to get back to work." She kisses me this time and starts to walk off.

I shake my head; my girl has some weird words that come from her delectable mouth. Awesomesauce. What kind of word is that? Oh, well. I turn myself and pick up my mug. Sipping my now lukewarm coffee I debate on what I will do for the rest of her shift.

I finish my coffee, pull out my wallet from my jeans pocket and lay a ten-dollar bill on the counter. The whole time I've been here, I only drank coffee, so I just left my girl a hefty tip. She will yell at me later, but then I'll get to punish her for it.

I look around for Devon to say goodbye to, but she's busy with customers, so I just head for the door.

The sun is shining. It's midafternoon now. The streets aren't very busy which is good. I'm not a fan of the whole hustle and bustle. From the corner of my eye, I notice a shadow hiding by a tree across the street. I can't help but look.

It's a quick glimpse, but I could swear I saw my brother Dom. I head in the direction of the tree. Looking both ways before crossing the street, I get to the tree. No one's there. Hmmph. They must have slipped away when I wasn't looking. But I swear it was my brother. Either that, or it's wishful thinking on my part. But then again if it was Dom, why is he hiding and being all sneaky like with me?

I look around. No one is close by so start walking. I'm two car lengths from the tree when a car door opens and someone steps out in front of me, stopping me dead in my tracks. Fuck. Pike.

With greasy, ripped jeans and a dirty white tank top on, he stands in front of me with his gun raised, pointing right at me. "Did you get your message?" He sneers.

Trying to think quick, but having no weapons of my own on hand, I raise my hands showing him I'm unarmed. "Yep." I respond. I shift my eyes to glance from side to side with hopes someone happens to notice what's happening and calls for help. But no such luck as I see no one. Shit.

"You have a sweet piece of ass of a woman. Cutting her up filled me with so much pleasure, I thought about leaving my other mark in her for you." He narrows his eyes and stares me down. The gun motionless.

Anger starts to build up. Fear of not being the good guy is out the window since he mentions Devon. He won't get the chance to fuck with her again. "Stay the fuck away from her." I growl. "Your beef is with me, asshole."

Pike waves the gun back and forth and snarls. "I needed to make a point to the all-powerful Jake Green."

"Point taken." I grunt.

I can't believe no one is outside to witness this. Fuck me, what luck I have. My shoulders grow tense. I want to attack him, but he has the gun. I have a reason to live so I have to try and work this out somehow.

Pike looks around and seems pleased. No one is watching. "No, Jake. Point not taken. Not until you're gone." He cocks the gun and re-aims. The trigger is pulled before I realize it because I'm hit. Searing sharp pain starts in my left chest and I collapse to my knees and fall to my back. Fuck.

A car door slams and tires peel off squealing as they go.

I grip my chest and press down. I can feel the blood spurting out and the pain is unbearable. Please God, let someone find me.

# JEAN KELSO

# CHAPTER THIRTY

*Devon*

"Order up." Mark calls from the window.

I rush up and grab the hot plate full of yummy poutine. My stomach growls hungrily. Poutine's one of my favorite foods and Mark makes a good one.

I snag a couple extra napkins and head over to the table that the order belongs to.

The lunch rush is long over and dinner rush starts early. A lot of my regulars have already shown up. I'm sure they were notified of my return to work as well. I'm still feeling good, considering how busy we have been.

I set the plate on the table and smile to the young woman. "Enjoy. Please let me know if you need anything else." I head back over to the bar and grab a bottled-water from the cooler.

The sound of a car backfiring rings loud and I drop my water. I look around the diner and everyone looks outside. People seem to be rushing about the sidewalk. Maybe it wasn't a car.

I'm the curious type of woman, so I pick up my bottle and set it on the bar. Wiping my hands on a dish towel, I head to the door.

Once outside I look around. People are starting to gather around in a group across the street. One guy has his phone to his ear, that means someone was shot. The two sounds are similar and scary.

I check for cars and rush across the street. If there's any way I can help, I will. I push myself through the crowd to see who was hit and my heart stops.

"Jake!" I yell. I drop to my knees and look over his still body. There's blood covering his chest and pooling on the ground. Tears start to pour out of my eyes and down my face. "No, Jake, you can't die on me." I look around the crowd. Everyone just stands there, watching. For what, I don't know.

I press my hands to his chest in search of the wound. I find it and press harder. I need the bleeding to stop. "Has anyone called nine-one-one yet?" I call out. I lean down and check to see if he is breathing. Thank fuck, he is.

"They are on their way, miss." Young male voice answers.

Using one hand I press on the bullet hole and with the other I assess him for other injuries. "Come on Jake, talk to me. Stay with me. Help is coming." I sob, my emotions in overdrive.

"Devon…" Jake gurgles, I barely hear him. I choke out another sob. He's alive. Now I just need to keep him that way.

With my bloody hand, I reach up and caress the side of his face. "Yeah, baby. I'm here."

I feel Jake moving slightly, his hand comes up slow and touches my face. I sniff, tears running like crazy. I can't lose him now. "Love you." His hand falls to the ground with a thud and his eyes close.

"Jake. Jake. JAKE!" I yell the last. His breathing stops and I think I lose my mind. "No. You're not dying today." I remember watching some old television shows where they did this chest thing to restart the heart, so like I said. Mind lost. I take in his still body and raise my arm, slamming it down with my hand in a fist, on his chest. Thump. "Not today, Jake." I do it again. Thump. "You are not dying." I scream through my cries.

Arms grab me by my shoulders and pull me back. "Let them help." A husky male voice tells me.

I struggle, fight, twist and turn in the man's arms. "Jake…" I cry out, the arms wrap around me and hold me tight.

Immediately paramedics rush in and start to work on him. They begin CPR and I can't watch. Grief strikes and I want to curl up and die right alongside him.

"We have a pulse. Get the gurney." A voice shouts.

What? He's not dead? My own pulse increases and I fight the restraining arms again. "Jake. Jake."

I turn in the arms wrapped around me and look right into the same eyes that I love so much. They look like Jake's eyes. But this man's not Jake. My breath catches and I stare. "How?" I mumble.

The man who looks like an older version of Jake, but has a large scar on his face and lighter hair grimaces at me. "I'm Dominic. His brother."

Chills run up my spine. This is the brother who's on the run. What's he doing here? Whatever, I can't think about that now, Jake's my concern. I turn to look over my shoulder. Jake is just getting put in the ambulance. "Hi." I whisper to Dom. As dumb as I sound, I don't care. I need to be with Jake. "Please let go. I want to go with him."

Dominic lets go, concern written on his face and I run after the paramedics. I notice Mark in the crowd that has grown in size and I know he knows. He nods and I hop in the back of the ambulance. "I'm his wife."

**I sit in** the waiting room of the intensive care unit. Jake was taken in for surgery and I was told he'd be brought here when they were done.

A police officer has been pacing the unit, waiting to see Jake. He doesn't look like he plans to leave anytime soon.

This is the second time Jake has been shot. I'm not sure I can handle any more drama like this. The police better deal with those men—and soon.

I'm tucked up on a chair, playing a scrabble like game on my phone when Sean walks in.

"Anything yet?" He asks. I called him and Jenn when I got here and Jake was rushed in for surgery.

I look up to him, setting my phone on the chair beside me. "Nothing yet." I frown.

Sean comes and sits beside me in the empty seat and wraps an arm around my shoulders. "He's a tough guy Devon. He'll pull through." He squeezes my shoulder—reassurance I think—and I try my hardest to believe him.

We sit in silence for a few minutes and I can't take it. My thoughts are wandering and I don't like where they take me. Licking my dry lips, I look to Sean. "I love him, Sean." I admit to him.

"What's not to love?" He looks at me with a smirk and then chuckles.

I hit him on the upper arm and giggle back. Man, I needed that. "You tool, Sean."

With a smile, he reaches over and pushes some hair behind my ear. "You needed a distraction woman, so I gave you one."

How right he is. What is it with the Green men? Sweet, sexy, and funny at all the right moments. Jenn's a lucky woman to have Sean. I just hope I luck out and get to keep Jake. The doors to the unit open and a stretcher being pushed by two attendants comes through.

I stand to get a better look. Jake. Finally, I reach for Sean and grab his hand. I need his support right now, and since he's his brother, he's the best support available.

# CHAPTER THIRTY-ONE

*Jake*

I open my eyes and everything's bright. Am I dead? Is this heaven? What am I saying? I wouldn't be in heaven. I don't know where I'd be, but not there. My eyes start to adjust and the light dims. My chest feels heavy and I'm rather groggy.

The last thing I remember is standing in front of Pike and then horrible pain. I got shot again. This time, I got shot good. Getting shot the first time didn't hurt that much. It was just a graze, a deep flesh wound of my arm. While it hurt enough, it was definitely nothing like this. I blink a few times and try to look around.

I'm in a room. It's plain, sterile like. Must be the hospital. There's someone sitting on a chair in the corner, actually two people. I blink a few more times to clear my fuzzy vision. Devon. Sean. I hear beeping and turn my head to see a big monitor on the wall with all kinds of funny squiggles and numbers. Looking down at myself, I see a hospital gown and an intravenous line coming from my arm. Yep, hospital for sure.

"Hey." I try to say, my throat dry, voice harsh. I try to swallow. It feels like a lump's there.

"He's awake." Devon rushes over to me. "Baby, how do you feel?" She asks.

I take a minute to assess my body and realize I'm in some pain. "I hurt." I grimace and look at her sweet face. She looks so worried. I can tell she has been crying. My sweet girl. I've scared her and it's something I never wanted to do.

"I'll get a nurse." I hear being told from behind her. Sean gets up and walks out of the room.

Devon looks me over and smiles a small smile. "I'm so happy you are alive. I thought I lost you." She reaches up and caresses the side of my face. A familiar feeling. Did she do this recently? I'm having a Deja Vu moment.

"I'm not ready to leave you, blondie." I tell her in hopes of showing her I'm going to be okay. Using her nickname, proving that no matter what I go through, I'm still me—and also to make her smile. I love this woman. I can see the fear, panic and love all etched in her eyes. It'd break her heart if I left her now.

She leans down and kisses my forehead. "Good. Now stop getting shot, damn it!" She spits out and tries to laugh it off. She doesn't do a good job of it.

"Yes, dear." I smirk and wince through my chuckle.

Devon narrows her eyes at me but smirks back. Yeah, I'm sure she knows I'm good. That *we're* good.

**I wake to** whispered voices in the room. I must've fallen asleep after receiving my pain medicine. The doctors always say rest is good for healing, so I just thought I'd rest my eyes and boom, I must've zonked. I glance around to see if I can tell what time of day it is, but I can't. So I try to focus on the voices. Looking in the direction, I see it's Devon and Dr. Godwin. Man, that doc gets around. I smile to myself. She must think we're a bunch of trouble makers.

I lie silently and listen.

"The bullet just missed his aorta and pulmonary artery. He was very lucky." This is spoken by the doc.

"Oh, my God." Devon puts her hand to her chest. "Was there complications in surgery?"

The doc shakes her head to the question and I feel relief. "No. I was able to retrieve the bullet, clean up the mess, and close him up. He did need to be transfused a couple units of blood. But other than that when he heals, he'll be good as new." Fuck, talk about a close call. I hear Devon sniffle and the doc pulls her in for a hug. Damn, the doc's a wonderful person—smart, classy and great with people. We owe her so much.

I clear my throat to get their attention and they both look my way.

"Hey, baby. You're awake. How do you feel?" Devon asks as she walks toward the bed with a smile on her beautiful face.

Returning her smile, I look to the doc and back to her. "Rested. Were you just talking about me?"

Devon blushes, such a beautiful site to be had and I can't help but grin. "Yes, we were. Dr. Godwin was updating me about you." She looks to the good doctor, so I do as well.

Dr. Godwin comes toward me, a big smile on her face, and leans against the end bed frame. "Yes, Mr. Green. I was just telling your lovely girl here that everything went well in surgery."

"That's great news. Can I go home now?" I smirk and watch the expressions on both women. Shock from both of them. I chuckle and hide my pain. "I'm kidding. I know I'll be here for a day or two."

"Try up to a week, Mr. Green." The doc says. Now it's time for *me* to go in shock. Like, what the fuck.

"A week?"

"Yes. I want to make sure everything is healing properly and that you don't get a post-operative infection." She stares at me, all serious and professional.

Well, fuck. I look to Devon and pout. "That sucks." Devon giggles.

Dr. Godwin laughs lightly at me or at Devon and I both. "You two are quite the pair. Anyways. If you need anything don't hesitate to ask. I'm going to continue on my rounds."

The doctor leaves and I blow out a breath. I really don't want to stay in the hospital for as long as she says, but if I have to I will.

I guess I did just get shot in the chest. Plus, I have a woman I need to live for—want to live for—so I better listen to the doctor.

I feel Devon wrap her hand around mine. I look down at our fingers tangled together and smile. Looking up at her, I see her bright eyes shine. "Hey." I whisper.

"Hey back."

"How are you holding up?" I ask. I know she hurts. The fact that we're sitting in this situation again, but the fact that I'm lying in the bed must be killing her. The last thing I ever wanted to do was hurt her. But here we are. My past is haunting us and I don't know when—or if—it'll ever stop.

"I've been better. But I'm glad to know you are going to back to normal soon." She rubs her thumb over the top of my hand. The tenderness she gives me is something no one has given me in a long time. Not since my mother.

"That's right, blondie. I'll have you on your back, naked and under me screaming my name in no time at all." I smirk. I can't let a bullet wound bring me down. I'm a man, aren't I?

Devon shakes her head and giggles. "Yep, there he is. My man." Her smile fades and a look of seriousness appears. "I met Dominic. He was there when the ambulance came."

Say what? Dominic is here? So I did see him, I'm not losing my mind. Fuck. He approached Devon. I sure hope he didn't hurt her. "Did he hurt you?"

# CHAPTER THIRTY-TWO

*Devon*

I scrunch my nose up and look at him. Why would his brother hurt me? I know he is on the run. Jake has told me a little about him, but still, for what reason would he hurt me? This I want answers for. "Why the hell would he hurt me?"

Jake closes his eyes and shakes his head. He opens his eyes and looks at me. "I don't know. I just worry about you is all."

It's nice to know he worries, but still, his brother has no reason to hurt me. Plus, if I was in danger, wouldn't Sean have told me? Maybe I should talk to him about it too. But that can wait til later if I feel I need to call at all.

I lift Jake's hand and give it a gentle kiss. "I'm good, Jake. He didn't hurt me. He seemed worried about you. Like a brother should, you know?"

"Well, it has been years since I have seen or heard from him. Didn't even know he was alive, that is how long it has been."

That's a long time. Maybe it's a good thing Dominic's here. A family reunion for the brothers might be a good thing. But then again—I don't know the man, and I don't really know how they all got along years ago. Only time will tell.

With Jake being hurt he won't be able to start work for a while, I don't like the fact of him living in the damn hotel like he has been. An idea comes to me, and I can't help but jump right on it.

"Hey, Jake? Move in with me." I don't ask. I just bluntly throw it out there. I don't plan on letting him go anytime soon. I'm in love with this man. Nothing about his past bothers me. To most people it would, but to me? I look at the person and see them for they really are. Jake definitely isn't the bad guy that people make him out to be. I can see him. He has good in him. He just needs that little something to help him pull it out. I can do that. Love can do that. I love him, so why not?

I watch the expression on his face and I can't make out what he's thinking. Is he nervous? Upset? Suddenly a huge smile is there. His eyes glisten. I swear he is going to cry, but he doesn't. Crying doesn't bother me. It only proves my theories about the good side of him.

"Do you really want that, blondie? Me—In your face twenty-four seven?" He smirks as if I asked him such a preposterous question.

I laugh lightly and bite my lip. Thinking back on our times together, I know I've told him I love him. But we only said it once, maybe twice. I'm not certain he really understands the depth of my feelings. With everything we both have been through in such a short time, the emotions have built up inside of me. I need to release them. Would now be the right time to tell him? Would he think I'm just saying it for the sake of saying it? I sure hope the fuck not.

"Jake. I love you. I have never loved someone the way I love you. So, yeah. I want you with me all the time. In my face, in my bed, in my body, screaming my name when we make love together." I can feel the heat rise up my neck to my cheeks. I'm happy I told him. Damn, that was hard. I'm not good with feelings or words, but it was easier than usual to say that to him.

Jake shifts his body in the bed and faces me. He tips his head suggesting that I move closer. "Come here, blondie."

I lean closer to him, just a hair's breadth apart from him.

"I love you too, Devon. More than I ever thought possible in this world." He pushes forward and presses his lips against mine in a warm, but gentle kiss sealing his confession.

A knock on the door startles us both and we look toward it.

Shock hits me. Dominic stands there. I look to Jake to see what he thinks and he appears to feel the same.

"Sorry to interrupt you both. I just wanted to check in on my little brother." Dominic says.

I look back to him and smile. I don't know what to expect, so I move from the bed and sit on the chair beside it. Dominic looks to me and then to Jake, uneasiness extrudes with his body language and shines in his eyes. I can tell he is unsure if it's a good idea to come here or not.

"Come on in, Dom." Jake tells him and Dominic walks in and stands at the end of the bed. Tension fills the room and I take a deep breath. I sure hope I'm not going to be a witness to an assault of any kind between brothers. Jake doesn't look overly happy, but then again, he could still be in shock. I haven't mastered all his looks yet.

Dom's tall, bulky and super sexy. Standing there with his dark wash jeans and tight shirt I can't help but do a once over. Fuck me. He's a bigger version of Jake. I feel I need to wipe my mouth from the drool that isn't actually there. Shaking my head, I look back to Jake and wait.

Dom smiles at me and looks back at Jake. "You have a stubborn girl there." He grips the bed tight as he talks. I can tell he's nervous. The years apart sure have taken its toll on these boys.

Jake finally grins, his whole mood shifts with talk about me. "Fucking right she is. I love her stubbornness. I get to punish her ass when she doesn't listen."

What? My eyes snap to him. "Jake!" I growl. How dare he freely tell his brother such personal information. I narrow my eyes at him when he looks at me and I glare. He just laughs.

"Relax, blondie. Dom may be a bad ass, but he's still my brother. I don't think he'll say anything to anyone. Shit, he has punished his fair share of chicks in the past—eh, Dom?" Jake looks at his brother, and Dom wears a shit eating grin.

Well, fuck me stupid. The whole band of brothers are nuts. I can't help but smirk at the pair of them. "Great." I say sarcastically and roll my eyes.

Jake and Dom both laugh. "See man? Punishment is fun with my girl. She likes to push buttons." Jake tells his brother.

"You look good, man." Dom tells Jake, his hands easing up from the bed. He steps over to a chair and sits down. "Fuck, it's been so long. I wish I could have visited you in prison, but you know…" He grimaces.

Jake nods. "You are a wanted man, Dom. I understand. Speaking of that, how are you here now?"

Dom looks to the door and back. "Got me some men watching out for me. Making sure I'm safe to be here until I leave."

"Leave?"

"Yeah, Jake. I got Sean's message, so I came. Can't stay, though. Got a new name, a job and all that shit up in Canada. Cleaned my shit up. I came for you and Sean. If I stay, who's to say I won't fall into old habits? And those old habits mean big trouble for all of us."

Well, shit. I feel a little mushy inside now. These big tough guys are softies. After living such rough lives, they all have turned themselves around proving people can change. I want to hug the big lug, but I won't. I don't want to make Jake jealous.

I sit back in my chair, get comfortable and listen. Jake and Dominic need to chat about life. I'm eager to learn every detail they're willing to share.

Dominic has been on the run for so long, but with such a loyal following no one has turned him in. A strong group of friends for sure. A brotherhood of sorts. Sure there are a few stragglers that need sorting, but he plans to take care of them.

Sean didn't have as many problems as Jake and Dominic and he did a full one-eighty and is living happily.

Dom told us that Pike and his brother Snake are no longer our problem—that they'll be taken care of before he leaves town. This helps seal the can of shit that's happening and makes me feel better.

The things I'm witnessing with this family, these brothers, I'm learning that anything is possible. With the life I've lived, the same city, the same job, going nowhere with my life, I know I can change it if I really want, but I'm content right now. I'm still young and I know have a good man. I'm happy.

The only thing I need to work forward with is helping Jake with his redemption. The one thing he craves and I know with absolute certainty he deserves.

JEAN KELSO

# EPILOGUE

*Jake*

It's been three months since I was shot. Seeing Dominic for the first time in years felt like he never left. He gave me a private email address that we can communicate through and he promised that we can meet up again sometime. I just hope that it's on good terms, for happy reasons, not because madmen are out for blood. It's something to look forward to.

Pike and Snake's bodies were found a week after Dom said his goodbyes to us. The police didn't even bother to investigate the situation (they figured it was drug related, an overdose of some sort) so I have pushed those names out of my mind. The only strange thing that haunts me is the other bodies that have been slowly popping up since Dom apparently left. I have a feeling that Dom may have fallen back in his old ways, either that or there's a new player in town. Either way, I'm going to have to prepare ahead of time just in case something happens. With my luck, you never know.

I'm moved in with my girl and things are great. My bullet wound is healed. I did some physiotherapy and only suffer from the occasional muscles stiffness in the surgical area.

I actually turned down the job that Mark and Devon offered me at the diner and started working with my brother Sean at his construction job. His forgiveness lifted the block that was weighing me down and I feel like a whole new man. Having my brother back means the world to me. Knowing Sean will have my back when in need, and I will have his, makes life feel right again.

I look at the clock and see it's almost five. Devon will be home at six. I need to get the lasagna out of the oven and hop in the shower. We are going to Sean and Jenn's for a potluck dinner tonight to celebrate. Jenn found out last week that she is two and half months pregnant with baby number two. Devon and I are doing a baby poll with everyone at the diner, placing bets on whether it's a girl or boy. Sean thinks we're idiots, but Jenn thinks it's awesome.

Devon and I both are hoping for a boy, this time. It's only fair Sofie gets a brother right?

The front door shuts and I hear keys hit the table. "Jake, I'm home. Mark let me leave early because of the party."

"In the kitchen, blondie." I call out as I pull the hot dish out of the oven and set it on top of the stove.

Footsteps patter in my direction and I turn. Devon has a big smile on her face. "Hey."

"Hey back." I smirk. "Any bets made today?" I ask. We have a huge board posted at the diner and if customers feel like placing a bet, they can just donate towards a gift for the expectant parents. We have pictures of Sean and Jenn on the board and Jenn's tiny baby bump that says, girl or boy. Devon made it and it actually looks pretty cool.

"Yeah, we had a couple. Everyone's saying a girl." She pouts.

I move to wrap my arms around her. I kiss her warm lips and smile. "Well, if she has a girl…" I bite my lip in a teasing way. "We'll just have to have a boy."

Devon looks up at me, a huge knowing grin on her face. "That we can do. Let's start now." She escapes my grasp and starts running for the bedroom.

Damn, I'm one lucky bastard. I run after her stripping my shirt off as I go.

THE END

# ABOUT THE AUTHOR

Jean is just a small town girl looking for a little adventure. With her love of reading and writing she wanted to explore and see what her characters could do for her. Being a nurse, a wife, and mother of two boys, she has her hands full, but takes the time to dream among the pages. She is a true blooded Canadian and hopes to explore parts of the world sometime in the future, but for now, she explores in the books she reads and writes. Being a huge Indie Author fan, she has made several friends online and has met a few at book signings. Hoping to one day meet some fans face to face, she would gladly friend you on Facebook, Goodreads, Twitter and Google+. She also has a website where you can order paperbacks and keep up to date on everything.

She can be found on Facebook: https://www.facebook.com/jean.kelso.14

She can be found on Goodreads: https://www.goodreads.com/author/show/8338589.Jean_Kelso

She can be found on Google+ as Barb Jean Kelso Johnson

Website: http://authorjeankelso.wix.com/authorjeankelso

Twitter: https://twitter.com/JeanKelsoAuthor